On Robert Holdstock:

'Britain's best fantasist … these are the visions of a real artist.' – *The Times*

'A new expression of the British genius for true fantasy.' – Alan Garner, on *Mythago Wood*

'A master fantasist' – *Guardian*

'Our finest living mythmaker. His narratives – intense, exuberant, earthy, passionate, dense with metaphor – are new trails through the ancient forest of our imaginations. An essential writer.' – Stephen Baxter

On Garry Kilworth:

'Arguably the finest writer of short fiction today, in any genre.' – *New Scientist*

'One of the most significant writers in the English language.' – *Fear Magazine*

'Probably one of the finest writers of short stories Britain has ever produced.' – *Bookstore Online*

'A master of his trade.' – *Punch Magazine*

WINNER OF THE WORLD FANTASY AWARD

THE RAGTHORN

ROBERT HOLDSTOCK
AND
GARRY KILWORTH

infinity plus

To Keith Brooke, a fine editor and publisher.

In memory of Rob Holdstock:

> *And though he faces away from us*
> *As he must*
> *His breath is the wind of life*
>
> RH

This edition copyright © 2015 Robert Holdstock and
Garry Kilworth

'The Ragthorn' copyright © 1991 Robert Holdstock and
Garry Kilworth
'The Fabulous Beast' copyright © 2013 Garry Kilworth
'The Charisma Trees' copyright © 1994 Robert Holdstock

Cover image © Willard
Cover design © Keith Brooke

All rights reserved.

Published by infinity plus
www.infinityplus.co.uk
Follow @ipebooks on Twitter

No portion of this book may be reproduced by any means, mechanical, electronic, or otherwise, without first obtaining the permission of the copyright holder.

The moral right of Robert Holdstock and Garry Kilworth to be identified as the authors of this work has been asserted by them in accordance with the Copyright, Designs and Patents Act of 1988.

ISBN-13: 978-1512281255
ISBN-10: 1512281255

CONTENTS

'The Ragthorn' by Robert Holdstock and Garry Kilworth 9
'The Fabulous Beast' by Garry Kilworth 65
'The Charisma Trees' by Robert Holdstock 91

The Authors 115
Acknowledgements 117

THE RAGTHORN

Robert Holdstock and Garry Kilworth

> Quhen thow art ded and laid in layme
> And Raggtre rut thi ribbis ar
> Thow art than brocht to thi lang hayme
> Than grett agayn warldis dignite.
>
> *Unknown* (c. A.D. 1360)

September 11, 1978

I AM PLACING THIS ENTRY at the beginning of my edited journal for reasons that will become apparent. Time is very short for me now, and there are matters that must be briefly explained. I am back at the cottage in Scarfell, the stone house in which I was born and which has always been at the centre of my life. I have been here for some years and am finally ready to do what must be done. Edward Pottifer is with me — good God-fearing man that he is — and it will be he who closes this journal and he alone who will decide upon its fate.

The moment is *very* close. I have acquired a set of dental pincers with which to perform the final part of the ritual. Pottifer has seen into my mouth – an experience that clearly disturbed him, no doubt because of its intimacy – and he knows which teeth to pull and which to leave. After the inspection he muttered that he is more used to pulling rose thorns from fingers than molars from jaws. He asked me if he might keep the teeth as souvenirs and I said he could, but he should look after them carefully.

I cannot pretend that I am not frightened. I have edited my life's journal severely. I have taken out all that does not relate forcefully to my discovery. Many journeys to foreign parts have gone, and many accounts of irrelevant discovery and strange encounters. Not even Pottifer will know where they are. I leave for immediate posterity only this bare account in Pottifer's creased and soil-engrimed hands.

Judge my work by this account, or judge my sanity. When this deed is done I shall be certain of one thing: that in whatever form I shall have become, I will be beyond judgement. I shall walk away, leaving all behind, and not look back.

Time had been kinder to Scarfell Cottage than perhaps it deserves. It has been, for much of its existence, an abandoned place, a neglected shrine. When I finally came back to it, years after my mother's death, its wood had rotted, its interior decoration had decayed, but thick cob walls – two feet of good Yorkshire stone – had proved too strong for the ferocious northern winters. The house had been renovated with difficulty, but the precious stone lintel over the doorway – the beginning of my quest – was thankfully intact and undamaged. The house of my childhood became habitable again, twenty years after I had left it.

From the tiny study where I write, the view into Scardale is as eerie and entrancing as it ever was. The valley is a sinuous, silent place, its steep slopes broken by monolithic black rocks and stunted trees that grow from the green at sharp, wind-shaped angles. There are no inhabited dwellings here, no fields. The only movement is the grey flow of cloud shadow and the flash of sunlight on the thin stream. In the far distance, remote at the end of the valley, the tower of a church: a place for which I have no use.

And of course – all this is seen through the branches of the tree. The *ragthorn*. The terrible tree.

It grows fast. Each day it seems to strain from the earth, stretching an inch or two into the storm skies, struggling for life. Its roots have spread farther across the grounds around the cottage and taken a firmer grip upon the dry stone wall at the garden's end; to this it seems to clasp as it teeters over the steep drop to the dale. There is such menace in its aspect, as if it is stretching its hard knotty form, ready to snatch at any passing life.

It guards the entrance to the valley. It is a rare tree, neither hawthorn nor blackthorn, but some ancient form of plant life, with a history more exotic than the

Glastonbury thorn. Even its roots have thorns upon them. The roots themselves spread below the ground like those of a wild rose, throwing out suckers in a circle about the twisted bole: a thousand spikes forming a palisade around the trunk and thrusting inches above the earth. I have seen no bird try to feed upon the tiny berries that it produces in mid-winter. In the summer its bark has a terrible smell. To go close to the tree induces dizziness. Its thorns when broken curl up after a few minutes, like tiny live creatures.

How I hated that tree as a child. How my mother hated it! We were only stopped from destroying it by the enormity of the task, since such had been tried before and it was found that every single piece of root had to be removed from the ground to prevent it growing again. And soon after leaving Scarfell Cottage as a young man, I became glad of the tree's defensive nature – I began to long to see the thorn again.

To begin with, however, it was the stone lintel that fascinated me; the strange slab over the doorway, with its faint alien markings. I first traced those markings when I was ten years old and imagined that I could discern letters among the symbols. When I was seventeen and returned to the cottage from boarding school for a holiday, I realised for the first time that they were cuneiform, the wedge-shaped characters that depict the ancient languages of Sumeria and Babylon.

I tried to translate them, but of course failed. It certainly occurred to me to approach the British Museum

– after all my great-uncle Alexander had worked at that noble institution for many years – but those were full days and I was an impatient youth. My study was demanding. I was to be an archaeologist, following in the family tradition, and no doubt I imagined that there would be time enough in the future to discover the meaning of the Sumerian script.

At that time all I knew of my ancestor William Alexander was that he was a great-uncle, on my father's side, who had built the cottage in the dales in 1880, immediately on his return from the Middle East. Although the details of what he had been doing in the Bible lands were obscure, I knew he had spent many years there, and also that he had been shot in the back during an Arab uprising: a wound he survived.

There is a story that my mother told me, handed down through the generations. The details are smudged by the retelling, but it relates how William Alexander came to Scarfell, leading a great black-and-white Shire horse hauling a brewer's dray. On the dray were the stones with which he would begin to build Scarfell Cottage, on land he had acquired. He walked straight through the village with not a word to a soul, led the horse and cart slowly up the steep hill to the valley edge, took a spade, dug a pit, and filled it with dry wood. He set light to the wood and kept the fire going for four days. In all that time he remained in the open, either staring out across the valley or tending the fire. He didn't eat. He didn't drink. There was no tree there at the time. When at last the fire died down he paid every man in the village a few shillings to help with the building of a small stone cottage. And one of the stones to be set — he told them — was a family tombstone whose faded letters could still be seen on its faces. This was placed as the lintel to the door.

Tombstone indeed! The letters on that grey-faced obelisk had been marked there four thousand years before, and it had a value beyond measure. Lashed to the deck of a cargo vessel, carried across the Mediterranean, through the Straits of Gibraltar, the Bay of Biscay, the obelisk had arrived in England (coincidentally) at the time Cleopatra's Needle was expected. The confused Customs officers had waved it through, believing it to be a companion piece to the much larger Egyptian obelisk.

This then is all I need to say, save to add that three years after the building of the cottage the locals noticed a tree of unfamiliar shape growing from the pit where the fire had burned that night. The growth of the tree had been phenomenally fast; it had appeared in the few short months of one winter.

The rest of the account is extracted from my journal. Judge me upon it. Judge my sanity. There are many questions to which there seem no answers. Who, or what, guided me to previously hidden information during the years? My uncle's ghost perhaps? The ghost of something considerably more ancient? Or even the spirit of the tree itself, though what would be its motive? There are too many coincidences for there *not* to have been some divine, some spiritual presence at work. But who? And perhaps the answer is: *no person at all*, rather a force of destiny for which we have no words in our language.

August 7, 1958
I HAVE BEEN AT TEL ENKISH for four days now, frustrated by Professor Legmeshu's refusal to allow me onto the site of the excavation. It is clear, however, that a truly astonishing discovery is emerging.

Tel Enkish seems to be the site of an early Sumerian temple to a four-part god, or man-god, with many of the attributes of Gilgamesh. From the small town of Miktah, a mile away, little can be seen but a permanent dust cloud over the low, dry hills, and the steady stream of battered trucks and carts that plough back and forth between the dump site and the excavation itself. All the signs are that there is something very big going on. Iraqi officials are here in number. Also the children of the region have flocked to Tel Enkish from miles around the site. They beg, they pester, they demand work on what is now known as "The Great Tomb". They are unaware that as a visitor I have no authority myself.

August 9, 1958
I HAVE AT LAST BEEN to the site. I have seen the shrine that William Alexander uncovered eighty years ago. I have

never in my life been so affected by the presence of the monumental past in the corroded ruins of the present.

My frantic messages were at last acknowledged, this morning at eight. Legmeshu, it seems, has only just made the connection between me and William Alexander. At midday, a dust-covered British Wolseley came for me. The middle-aged woman who drove it turned out to be Legmeshu's American wife. She asked me, "Have you brought the stone?" and looked around my small room as if I might have been hiding it below the wardrobe or something. She was angry when I explained that I had brought only my transcription of the glyphs on the weathered rock. She quizzed me as to where the stone was now located, and I refused to answer.

"Come with me," she snapped, and led the way to the car. We drove through the jostling crowds in silence. Over the nearest rise we passed through barbed-wire fencing and checkpoints not unlike those to be found in army camps. Iraqi guards peered into the vehicle, but on seeing Dr. Legmeshu waved us on. There was a sense of great agitation in the air. Everyone seemed tense and excited.

The site itself is in a crater of the tel, the mound on which the temple had been built and over which later generations of buildings in mud had been added. In the fashion of the notorious archaeologist Woolley, the top layer of the tel had been blasted away to expose the remains of the civilisation that had flourished there in the third millennium B.C. It had not been Legmeshu who had been so destructive, but my ancestor, Alexander.

As I feasted my eyes on the beautifully preserved building, she waited impatiently. She told me that the temple was from the period associated with Gilgamesh the King. It was made of refined mud-brick, and had been covered with a weatherproof skin of burnt brick set in bitumen.

"Where had the Alexander stone been set?" I asked, and she pointed to the centre of the ruins. "They had created a megalith structure at the very heart of the temple. The stone that your relative stole was the keystone. This is why you must return it. We cannot allow ..." She broke off and looked at me angrily. If she had been about to make a threat, she had thought better of it.

Her attitude led me to expect the worst from the male Dr. Legmeshu, but I am delighted to say that he could not have been more charming. I found him in the tent, poring over a set of inscriptions that had been traced out on paper. He was leaning on a large slab of rock and when I looked more closely I saw that it was identical to the lintel at Scarfell Cottage.

He was fascinated by the route I had taken in discovering him. The Iraqi government had made formal representation to the British government, five years before, for the return of the "Tel Enkish Stone" to its natural site. Unlike the Elgin Marbles, which the British Museum regarded as their right to keep safe, no official in London had ever heard of the Tel Enkish Stone.

The argument had waged within those same "scenes" for years, and had finally been taken up by the press. A picture of one of the other Tel Enkish stones had caught my attention, along with the headline: WHERE IS THE ALEXANDER STONE? Some keen reporter had obviously done his research to the point where he had made the connection.

The museum by that time had established that the stone had been removed by Professor Alexander, who they understood had retired to an unknown location after returning from the Middle East in the late 1890s. The Iraqi government believed none of this of course, thinking that the British Museum had the stone hidden, and relations were soured between the two countries for some years afterwards.

I have told Legmeshu that the stone lies in a quarry, the location of which I shall make known to the museum on my return to the United Kingdom. He has accepted this.

The story of those events, eighty years before, is difficult to ascertain. Alexander had worked on the site with Legmeshu's own great-grandfather. The two men had been close friends, and had made the astonishing discovery of the megaliths at the heart of the mud-brick temple together. There had been eight stones arranged in a circle, standing vertically. Four stones had lain across their tops.

A mini Stonehenge. And in the centre, four altars, three to known gods, one ... one that defied explanation.

"No trace of those altars remains," Legmeshu told me over tea. "But my great-grandfather's notes are quite clear. There were three altars to the three phases of the Hunter God: the youth, the king, the wise ancient. But to whom the fourth altar was dedicated ...?" He shrugged. "A goddess perhaps? Or the king reborn? My relative left only speculation."

There had been a difference of opinion during that first excavation; a fight; and a death. Apart from what I have written here, the record is blank, save for a folk memory from the inhabitants of Scarfell concerning a tree that grew one winter – a black and evil-looking thorn.

Legmeshu snatched my copy of the Scarfell inscription. He ran his eyes over the signs, the cuneiform script that seemed as familiar to him as was my own alphabet to me. "This is not all of it," he said after a long while. I had realised some time before that the fourth surface of the stone, flush with the brickwork between door and ceiling, had characters on it like the other three. They could not be read of course without demolishing the cottage, which I had not been prepared to do at the time. I told Legmeshu that the fourth side had been exposed over a long period to the toxic air of a northern English factory town and the characters had been all but erased.

He seemed beside himself with fury for a moment. "What a destructive and stupid thing to do, to leave the stone in such a place. It *must* be returned! It *must* be rescued!"

"Of course," I said. "I intend to do so on my return to England. I have only just located the stone myself, after years of studying my great-uncle's notes ..."

He seemed mollified by this. I have no intention of giving up the whereabouts of the stone however. I lie without shame. I feel obsessively protective towards the stone ... towards the cottage, and yes, in my adulthood, towards the tree. Somehow they are linked through my great-uncle and to remove or destroy any one of them would be like smashing the Rosetta Stone with a sledge hammer.

Legmeshu seemed to come to a sudden decision, saying, "Follow me," and led me down to the site itself. We came at last to the wide tarpaulin that covered the centre of the temple.

It was an area of mystical energy. I could sense the presence of invisible power. It had an immediate and lasting effect on me. I began to shake. Even as I write – hours after the experience – my hand is unsteady. As I stood there I was in the far past. Fingers of time brushed through my hair; the breath of the dead blew gently against my face. Sounds, smells, touches ... and an overwhelming, awe-inspiring *presence* – silently watching me.

Legmeshu seemed entirely unaware of these things.

His voice brought me back to the present. He was pointing to the small concrete markers that now showed where the stones had stood, in a circle about twenty feet in diameter. On the floor, clearly outlined in the dry mud, were the twisting impressions of roots.

"It was open to the sky," Legmeshu said. "In the centre of the stones a tree had been grown, quite a large tree by the looks of it. The four altars were orientated east-west. We think there may have been a mud-filled pit below the trunk of the tree, to support its growth."

"And the purpose of the place?" I asked. Legmeshu smiled at me and passed me a small book. I opened it and saw that he had written out the translations from each stone. The partial content of the Alexander stone had just been added and I studied the stilted English. Almost immediately I was aware of what I was reading.

Legmeshu's breathless, "It includes much of the original epic that has been lost, and earlier forms of the rest. It is a momentous find!" was quite unnecessary. I was lost in words:

> And behold the waters of the Flood were gone. The mud covered the land as a cloak which stifles. Gilgamesh waited on a hill and saw Utnapishtim, Boatman of the Flood, rise from the plain of mud and beckon. "Gilgamesh I shall reveal to you a secret thing, a mystery of the gods. Hark my words. There is a tree that grows from fire under the water, under the mud. It has a thorn prick, a rose blade on every twig. It will wound your hands, but if you can grasp it, then you will be holding that which can restore youth to a man. Its name is Old Man Who Would Be

Young." "How deep is the mud?" Lord Gilgamesh asked. "Seven days and seven nights," answered the Boatman, and Gilgamesh drew breath, and swam into the blackness.

When he had cut Old Man Who Would Be Young he swam again to the surface of the mud. Utnapishtim sent a woman with golden tresses to clean and anoint the body of the kingly man. And Gilgamesh possessed her for seven days and seven nights in a fury of triumph, and not for one moment did he let go of Old Man Who Would Be Young. And when the child was born, Utnapishtim gave it at once to Old Man Who Would be Young, so that the first berry appeared on the branches. "Now it will grow," the Boatman said. "And I have told you of the temple you must build and the manner of anointing the flesh."

Now Gilgamesh departed for high-walled Uruk, and when the thorns of Old Man Who Would Be Young pricked his thumbs he was increased of power. And he denied all the old men their touch of the tree, so that their youth was denied them. But when the time came, Gilgamesh alone would place Old Man Who Would Be Young in the proper way, and lie with it in an embrace of seven days and seven nights.

Here then, carved in stone, was a version of the immortality tale of *The Epic of Gilgamesh* that was quite unlike the story from the clay tablets. And it was an *earlier* version, Legmeshu was quite adamant, a cruder form, with hints of the magic ritual that the later version appears to have lost.

"The stone came from Egypt," Legmeshu said. "This place functioned as a ritual site of enormous importance for perhaps two hundred years. The secret plant seems to have been a thorn, which would account for the pattern of roots on the mud there. I believe this place celebrated immortality. And the fourth altar may be representational: the risen life. So we have Youth, King, Magus, and again Youth."

Legmeshu spoke, but his words became just sounds. He seemed more interested in archaeology than in the astonishing *literary* discovery. To him, legends are only part of the story of the people; they are one more tool, or one more part of the machine that is archaeology. He wants the words intact, as much as he wants the stone intact, but I realise now that he has not been affected by the *meaning* of the words, neither their literal interpretation nor what they imply about culture and ritual in the earliest of civilised times.

Quite clearly my great-uncle was! What other reason could there have been for his dragging away one of the stones – the key stone – and raising, too, a strange and gloomy tree. Did he find the seed of a familiar thorn that in the time of Babylon was known as Old Man Who Would Be Young?

The key! It tells of the growth from fire of a tree. It tells of the child who must be given to the growing sapling.

And what other salient information lies on the hidden face of the lintel, awaiting discovery?

August 10, 1958
I CAN STAY HERE NO longer. I wish to return to the site at Tel Enkish but I have received word that the Iraqis are unhappy that I "own" the stone. The time has come to slip away from this country. For a while, anyway. I leave so much unfinished; I leave so many questions unanswered.

June 14, 1965
I HAD ALMOST COME TO believe that my supernatural encounter at Tel Enkish was no more than imagination; whimsy. The intervening years have been very barren and very frustrating. (Legmeshu has finally ceased to hound me for the stone, but I still watch my back whenever I am in the Near or Middle East.) Now, something has turned up and I have flown to Cairo from Jerusalem (via Cyprus).

It began two months ago. I was in Jerusalem, initiating the project for which Cambridge has at last agreed to fund me; namely, to identify and discover the true symbolic and mythological meaning of the type of tree that provided the Crown of Thorns at Christ's execution. (A briar wreath, a coif of knotted thistles, a halo of thorn tree twigs? From what species of shrub or tree?) The reference to the "resurrecting thorn" in the work of the unknown writer of Gilgamesh has haunted me for years. Of all the world's great resurrections, Christ's is the most famous. I am increasingly obsessed with the true manner of that raising, and the Crown of Thorns is a teasing symbol, a provocative invitation that came to me while staring at the ragthorn through the window of Scarfell Cottage.

One afternoon, in the university library canteen, a noisy crowded place, I overheard a conversation.

The two men were behind me, speaking in awkward English, obviously a second language to them both. One of them was an Israeli diplomat I recognised; the other was an Arab. I guessed from the dialect of his occasional exclamations in his first language, that he was Egyptian. Their conversation was hushed, but I could hear it quite clearly, and soon became intrigued.

The Egyptian said, "Some diving men, with the tanks on the back – not professional men – tourist. They are swim near Pharos Island, where sunk the old light warnings for ships …"

The Israeli took a moment to work out what was being said.

"Light warnings? Light*house*. The Pharos lighthouse?"

The Egyptian said excitedly, "Yes, yes! By ancient city Alexandria. Yes. Find some very old jar. Very old. Thousands years. No sea get into jar. Papers inside. Old papers. Old before coming of Roman peoples. Many more jars in sea, so I am told."

Their voices dropped even lower and I found it was hard to catch what was being said. All I could determine was that the Israeli government are interested in any scroll that relates to its own culture. Naturally, they are prepared to pay a great deal of money and the Egyptian was busy lining his own pockets by bringing this information to the attention of the Israeli Ministry of Culture.

The thought occurred to me immediately: Might there be something in the jars that relates to the *thorn?*

It has been years since Tel Enkish, but once again I have a feeling of fate unfolding: of being watched by the silent past. I am convinced there is something in Cairo for *me.*

June 19, 1965
MY CONTACT HERE IS ABDULLAH RASHID. He is well known to the professors at the University in Jerusalem and has "supplied" objects and information to them for some years.

Professor Berenstein in Jerusalem is a friend of mine and kindly arranged the surreptitious meeting with this man who is in a position to inspect and copy the contents of the jars. This morning, after "checking my credentials", Abdullah came to my hotel. Over breakfast he explained that five of the ancient jars had already been taken from the water and two of them opened in controlled conditions. He is cagey about his knowledge of the contents, but has remarked, cryptically, that he believes there *is* a reference to some thorn tree amongst the first papers to be removed and examined.

The discovery is, as I knew, being kept under tight wraps, and Abdullah was surprised and impressed that I managed to hear about the parchments. It is the intention of the Egyptians to translate the documents and plays themselves, and take full credit before releasing the finds to the world at large. Hence, people like Abdullah are making a great deal of money leaking facsimiles of the parchments.

This is what Abdullah has told me: The discovery so far is of several documents that survived the fire in the Library of Alexandria two thousand years ago. The belief is that before the rioting crowd managed to penetrate the library, strip its shelves, and set the place alight, a number of soldiers loaded saddlebags with whatever the librarians could select to save, and rode from the city to a galley, which pulled offshore. Here, forty glazed amphorae were filled with manuscripts and sealed with wax, linen, more wax, and finally corked with clay. For some reason the jars were thrown overboard near the lighthouse. Perhaps the crew suddenly found themselves in danger and unable to set sail? Nothing more is known of this. Certainly the intention would have been to recover the vessels, once the danger was past, but it must be surmised that there were no survivors who knew of the whereabouts of the jars, nor even that they existed. Seawater rotted the rope nets holding them together and then currents carried some of the jars out into the Mediterranean, and stretched them in a line towards Cyprus.

June 20, 1965

TODAY WE SAW THE RECOVERY operation at work. The shores of Alexandria are always bustling with small craft, mostly feluccas similar to that in which we serenely approached the island. We blended well, since I had dressed in local fashion. It was calm on the blue waters, but the sun bore down on us with unrelenting pressure and its effects have made me quite dizzy. We sailed to Pharos Island, to the northern point, and watched a large rusty dredger assist a team of divers in bringing up the precious artifacts.

Eventually we received our reward. We saw one of the amphorae winched from the water. It was long and slender, encrusted with limpets and barnacles, and dripped a particularly silky, dark green weed, which hung from the bullet-blunt jar like a beard. A crab of gigantic size dangled from this furze by one claw, as if reluctant to release the treasure that had for so long been the property of the ocean.

I asked Abdullah where the amphora would now be taken. He told me, "To the museum." There it would be opened in controlled conditions.

"Is there no chance I could witness the opening?"

He shook his head and laughed. He told me that only certain government ministers and professors would be there. And some technical assistants, who were highly trusted.

Again the laughter as he prodded his chest.

"People like me," he said.

Abdullah's work would be to photograph the opening of the jars, at each stage, then any contents, page by page. Facsimiles would be made from the photographs.

"These facsimiles would be for sale?"

"Not officially of course" – he smiled – "but all things are negotiable, yes?"

June 23, 1965
ABDULLAH WAS HERE, BUT THE news is not good. He has been unable to obtain copies yet, not just for me but for others, as he must not be caught compromising his position at the museum. He has photographed several manuscripts so far.

It is a mixed bag, apparently, and includes two pieces by Plato, a play by Flatus called *Servius Pompus,* and twenty pages of a manuscript by Julius Caesar, entitled *His Secret Dialogues with the Priests of Gaul on the Nature of their Magic and Rituals.*

The final piece of parchment contains an even more exquisite original hand: that (it is believed) of Homer himself. It is a fragment of his *Iliad,* and consists of half of the Death of Hector, all the Funeral of Patroclus, and a third or so of the Funeral Games. It is a manifestly ancient hand, and the Egyptians are quite convinced that it *is* the writings of Homer, adding weight to the argument that Homer was one man, and not a collective of writers.

All of this would be enough to excite me beyond tolerance, but Abdullah, aware of the nature of my search, has now told me something that holds me breathless in anticipation: that the *Iliad* fragment contains reference to a "blood thorn".

That is the facsimile I want. I have told him that no matter what else he obtains, he *must* get that fragment of unknown Homer. My enthusiasm has no doubt put up the price of those lines of verse, but I am sure I am being skilfully teased into such a state by Abdullah. He could probably produce the goods now, but is jigging the price up with his procrastination, pretending he is being watched too closely. I can play the game too, and have let him see me packing my suitcase, and looking anxiously at my diary.

October 1, 1965
I AM BACK AT THE cottage in Scarfell, the place of my birth. I have come here because I *feel* I have been summoned home. I have been at Cambridge for most of the summer, but the voice of something dark, something omnipresent, has called me here ... home to the cottage, to the wild valley, to the tree.

I have translated much that Abdullah was able to sell me. And indeed, the documents make fascinating reading.

The "new" play by Titus Maccius Plautus (200 B.C.) is hilarious. *Servius Pompus* is completely typical, dealing with a common legionary in Fabius's army who is convinced he is of noble birth, and treats his comrades like dirt. His ultimate discovery that he is slave-born earns him a permanent position: on a cart, collecting the dung left behind by Hannibal's elephants.

The fragment of Caesar is most atypical however and very strange, detailing as it does the legendary and magic matter of the Celtic inhabitants of Europe, and there is a fascinating revelation concerning the coded language that existed within the arrangement of the stones on the landscape.

All that is for another paper. For the moment, it is the Homeric verse that excites me, for in this fragment of the epic cycle of the Greeks on the shores of Asia Minor there is a reference to the resurrection that confirms me in two beliefs: that there has been a deliberate effort to obliterate this knowledge from the world, and that someone – or some *thing* – is guiding my search to build again that knowledge from the clues I am gradually discovering.

The autumn day is dark as I write this, with huge columns of thunderous cloud drifting over Scarfell from the west. I am working by lamplight. I am chilled to the bone. The great rugged face of the fell surrounds me, and the solitary thorn – black against the darkness – seems to lean towards me through the small leaded windows that show its sinister form. That tree has known eternity, I sense now that it has seen me learn of Achilles, and *his* unsure use of the ancient magic.

Here then is my crude translation of the passage of the *Iliad* that is relevant. It is from the "Funeral of Patroclus",

Achilles's great friend. While Achilles sulked in his tent, during the siege of Troy, Patroclus donned the man's armour and fought in his place, only to be killed by the Trojan hero Hector. After Patroclus's body had been burned on the funeral pyre ...

> *... then they gathered the noble dust of their comrade*
> *And with ashes from the fire filled a golden vase.*
> *And the vase was double-sealed with fat*
> *Then placed reverently in the hut of the gallant Patroclus,*
> *And those who saw it there laid soft linens*
> *Over the gold tomb, as a mark of respect.*
> *Now the divine Achilles fashioned the barrow for his friend.*
> *A ring of stone was laid upon the earth of the shore*
> *And clear spring water was sprinkled amongst the stones.*
> *Then rich dark soil was carried from the fields and piled upon the stones.*
> *Until it was higher than the storm-soaked cedar.*
> *Prince Achilles walked about the barrow of Patroclus*
> *And wept upon the fertile ground which held his friend*
> *While Nestor, son of Neleus, was sent a Dream from Heaven.*
> *The Dream Messenger came from Zeus, the Cloud-compeller*
> *Whose words reached the ears of the excellent Achilles*
> *Who pulled the blood thorn from the wall of Troy*
> *And placed the thorn tree on the tear-soaked mound.*
> *In its branches he placed the sword and shield of Patroclus*
> *And in so doing pierced his own flesh with the thorn,*
> *Offering lifeblood as his blood for life.*

Here, the fragment returns to the story content as we know it: the funeral games for Patroclus and the final reckoning between Achilles and the Trojan champion, Hector. My translation leaves a great deal to be desired.

The *metre* of Homer's verse in the original seems very crude, not at all as we have become used to it, and perhaps later generations than Homer have "cleaned up" the old man's act, as it were. But there is power in the words, and an odd obsession with "earth". When Homer wrote them, I am sure he was powered by the magic of Zeus, a magic that Achilles had attempted to invoke.

Poor Achilles. I believe I understand his error. The whole ritual of the burial, of course, was intended to *bring Patroclus back to life!*

His mistake was in following the normal Mycenaean custom of burning the body of his friend upon the pyre. Patroclus never rose again. He couldn't. It is apparent to me that Zeus tried to warn him *not* to follow custom, *not* to place the body of his friend upon the burning faggots, because several lines previously (as the body of Patroclus was laid upon the pyre), Homer had written:

> *Now in the honouring of Patroclus there was unkind delay,*
> *No fire would take upon the wood below the hero.*
> *Then the excellent Achilles walked about the pyre and mourned anew*
> *But through his grief-eyes he saw the answer to the fire*
> *And raised his arms and prayed to all the winds*
> *And offered splendid sacrifice to the two gods*
> *Boreas from the North and Zephyr of the Western Gale.*
> *He made them rich libations from a golden cup*
> *And implored them blow among the kindling*
> *So that the honouring fire might grow in strength and honoured ash be made of brave Patroclus.*

No fire would take and Achilles failed to see the chance that his god was offering him. Zeus was keeping the wind from the flames, but seeing his warnings go unheeded, he turned away from Achilles in a passing pique.

Nothing else in this fragment seems to relate to the subject of the thorn, nor its means of operation. Abdullah has promised to send me more material when and if he can, but since nothing has arrived for several months, already I suspect that the knowledge of the lost amphorae and their precious contents is being suppressed.

What can I learn from Homer? That there was a genuine belief in the power of the *thorn* to raise the dead? That some "pricking of the flesh" is important? Achilles pricks his arm: his blood for life. But this is not the only life hinted at in the two references I have so far found: a child was given to the tree, according to the Gilgamesh fragment.

I feel the darkness closing in.

March 11, 1970
THE STONE LINTEL IS *BOUND* to the tree! Bonded to it. Tied! It is a frightening thought. This morning I tried to dislodge the stone from its position, scraping at the cement that binds it to the rest of the coarse stone of the cottage. I discovered that the ragthorn's roots are *in the house itself!* It is clear to me now that my great-uncle had a far better understanding of the importance of the tree and stone than I have so far imagined. Why did he drag back the

Gilgamesh stone to England? Why did he embed it in the way he did: as part of a door, part of a house? Is the "doorway" symbolic? A divide through which one passes from one world to another? Obviously the hidden side of the lintel contains words of great importance, words that he decided had to be concealed from the curious eyes of his contemporaries. The stone is not a tomb's marker, it is the tomb itself: the tomb of lost knowledge!

All this has occurred to me recently and this morning I began to extract the lintel from its resting place. I used proper tools and a great deal of brute strength. Imagine my surprise when I discovered that I was scraping through *plant tissue!* A thorny root stabbed out at me, then hung there, quivering and slowly curling. It has frightened me deeply. The whole lintel is covered and protected – on its hidden face – by an extension from the ragthorn that grows at the end of the garden, a menacing and evil presence. I could sever the root to the cottage, but I feel a chill of fear on each occasion that I ponder this possibility. Even now, as I write, I feel I am drawing a terrible darkness closer.

The tree has come to inhabit the house itself. There is a thick tendril of dark root running along the wall in the kitchen.

The chimney stack is webbed with tree roots. I lifted a floorboard and a thin tendril of the ragthorn jerked away from the sudden light. The floor is covered with tiny feelers.

Webbed in tree. And all centring on the stone lintel, the ancient monolith.

No wonder I feel watched. Was it my uncle's doing? Or was he merely obeying the instructions of a more sinister authority?

September 22, 1970
I HAVE RECEIVED A MESSAGE from the British Museum, forwarded from my rooms in Cambridge by my research assistant, David Wilkins. He alone knows where I live. He is an able student, a keen researcher, and I have confided in him to a considerable degree. On my behalf he is searching the dusty archives of Cambridge for other references to the "ragthorn" or to resurrection. I am convinced that many such references must exist, and that it is a part of my new purpose to elicit them, and to use them.

"Has the museum any record of William Alexander, or any knowledge of the whereabouts of his papers?" I had asked in 1967, without result.

The new letter reads quite simply thus: "We have remembered your earlier enquiry concerning the effects, records, papers, and letters of William Alexander and are pleased to inform you that a small string-bound, wax-sealed file has been discovered, a fragment of his known effects that has clearly been overlooked during the process of reinstatement of said effects to the rightful owner. We would be most pleased to offer you the opportunity to break the seal on this file, and to review the contents, prior to discussing a mutually suitable arrangement for their final disposal."

September 25, 1970

I WONDER NOW WHETHER OR not William Alexander *intended* this file to be discovered. I would like to think that in his aging bones, he felt someone coming behind, a soulmate, a follower who would become as entranced with his work as he was himself. Considering what I believe now, however, I think it more likely that he intended at some time to recover the file in person, and perhaps *after* most people believed him gone.

Today I have spoken to my great-uncle. Or rather ... he has spoken to me. He is as close to me now, as I sit here in my room in the Bonnington Hotel writing these notes, as close to me as if he were here in person. He has left a fragment of his work, a teasing, thrilling fragment.

What did he do with the rest of his papers? I wonder.

The man was born in 1832. There is no record of his death. The year is 1970. It is autumn. I tremble to think of this, but I wonder if a man, born before the reign of Victoria had begun, is still walking abroad, still soaking up the rain and the wind and the sun of the England that birthed him, or of the Bible lands that so captured his heart?

This is a summary, then, of the day's events and discoveries: This morning I entered the labyrinthine heart of the British Museum: those deep dark corridors and rooms that have been burrowed into the bruised London clay below the building. I was conducted to a small book-lined room, heavy with history, heady with the smell of parchment and manuscript. A man of sober demeanour and middle age received us. He had been working under a single pool of desk lamplight, imprisoned by it like some frugal monk. On my arrival he favoured me with room lighting, so that his desk was no longer a captive of the lamp. He was, despite his dour looks, a cheerful soul, and was as delighted by his discovery of William Alexander as I would become of my discovery of his remaining notes. Alexander, it seems, was an old rogue. He had a formidable reputation. He was known as an eccentric man, of extravagant tastes, and frontiers-man's manners. He had shocked the denizens of the nineteenth-century archaeological establishment with his rough Yorkshire speech, his outlandish manners. If it were not for the fact that he produced priceless historical artifacts from lands closed to most Europeans, he might have been ostracised by society from the outset.

He had, it seemed, collected his papers and belongings from his private offices in the deep recesses of the museum, on the 15th March, 1878. His departure had been quite typical of the man. He had placed his files and books upon a handcart and hauled it, clattering, up the levels, dragging it through the reading room disturbing everyone present, through the wide foyer, and out into the day, having caused more than one jowl in the establishment to quiver with indignation. He used to tell my mother, with a hearty chuckle, that if the Victorians were good at one thing, it was displaying indignation.

On passing the Chief Curator on the steps outside, he reached into a bag, drew out a vase of exquisite Egyptian design, and passed it over. When opened, within the neck of the previously sealed vase was a perfectly preserved red rose, its scent a fleeting moment of an ancient summer's day, instantly lost as the flower became dust.

Not on the cart that day, however, were thirty sheets of paper, loosely bound between two stiff pieces of cardboard (marked with his initials) and tied with string, He had placed a red wax seal across each of the round edges of the sheaf. On being handed the package, I slit the seals and cut through the formidable string knot with my penknife: shades of an Alexander who lived long before William.

Most of the sheets in the folio are blank. I shall summarise the puzzling contents of the rest.

Sheet 21. This consists of the single word: REVELATION!

Sheet 22. This is written in a more precise hand, but clearly William Alexander's. It reads: "The Bard too! The knowledge passed down as far as ELZBTH 1st. Who censored it? Who changed the text? Two references are clear, but there must be more. There *must* be. Too sweet a myth for WAS to ignore. P – has discovered lost folio, but spirited it away." (Two sheets covered with numbers and letters: a code of some sort?)

Sheet 25. This is headed "The Dream of the Rood". It is one of two sheets that clearly relates to the "thorn" and "resurrection". The margin of this sheet is peppered with words from the Anglo-Saxon language, but the main body of Alexander's text reads like this: *"Sige-beam."* This means Victory tree? The runic character "thorn" is used more prolifically in the alliterative half-lines than seems usual around this point in the poem's body. Then the word *swefna:* "of dreams". Then there are the words *syllicre treow:* "wonderful tree". This phrase is enclosed by the rune "thorn". A dream tree, a tree of victory (victory over death?) *surrounded and protected by thorns.*

"Yes." *The tree of everlasting life.* The tree is the *rood,* of course, the symbol of Christ's cross. But surely "tree" is meant in another sense too? A literal sense. Then, to confirm this, the phrase in the poem "adorned with coverings". Perhaps this means more than it says? Perhaps strips of material? *Rags?*

"I am certain that the message here is the *ragthorn tree.*"

This is the only note on *The Dream of the Rood* in my great-uncle's file, but it proves that *some,* albeit cryptic, references to the ragthorn remain extant, since this text can be read in any school edition of the poem.

It is clear that an abiding and darker myth concerning the return to life of a soul "buried beneath a tree" has been imposed upon the Christianity of the author (who probably wrote the "Rood" in the eighth century). But was the ragthorn at that time a tangible shrub that could be plucked, planted, and left to resurrect the corpse of the thane or lord buried below? Or was it already a myth by that time in Old England?

The last sheet contains two fascinating pieces of Middle English poetry, dating from the late 1300s, I would think, as one of them is the last stanza of Chaucer's famous poem *The House of Fame*, believed to be unfinished. It is clear that the poem *was* completed, but the last few lines removed, either by Chaucer himself, or by orders of his patron.

Alexander, who must have discovered the parchment, though it is not part of his file, had this to say:

"It is Chaucer's script, no doubt about it. The parchment page is faded, the ink has spread, but I am certain this is the original. Other editions omit the final four lines. Here they are, following the *known* ending:

Atte laste y saugh a man,
Which that y (nevene) nat ne kan
But he seemed for to be
A man of gret auctorite ... (here the known MS ends)
Loo! how straungely spak thys wyght
How ragethorn trees sal sithe the night,
How deeth sal fro the body slynke
When doun besyde the rote it synke.

To put those last few lines into more familiar language: Lo, this man spoke of strange things, of ragthorn trees scything away the darkness and how death will creep away from the body if it is buried beneath the ragthorn's roots.

Finally, a single stanza from an English religious lyric, which my great-uncle found at the same time:

> *Upon thys mount I fand a tree*
> *Wat gif agayne my soule to me!*
> *Wen erthe toe erthe of mortual note*
> *And ssulen wormes feste in thi throte*
> *My nayle-stanged soule will sterte upriss*
> *On ssulen wormes and erthe to piss.*

> (On this hill I found a tree
> which gave me back my (soul) –
> While the world might take note of mortality
> And sullen worms feast on your throat,
> My thorn-pierced body will rise up
> To treat the worms and the world with contempt.)

This, then, concludes my listing of the sheets bound into what I shall call "The Alexander Folio". How much further in his quest my great-uncle managed to journey is hard to know, but he certainly discovered more than have I. What fire must have burned within him. What a fever of discovery!

How death shall from the body slink when down beside the root it sinks...

That tree. That terrifying tree. It is the route to and from the Underworld for a man who is reluctant to die, who wishes to remain ... *immortal.*

October 13, 1971

I AM BEING DIRECTED, OR drawn, towards new discoveries. Is it my great-uncle? Or the tree? If it is William Alexander, then he must be dead, for the spirit of a living man would not work this way. It is only spirits that have been freed from mortality that can guide the living.

This leaves me wondering about whether Alexander attempted immortality – and *failed?*

I suspect that if I searched the grounds of Scarfell Cottage carefully, or dug below the walls, into the space below the tree, I believe I would find his bones. Is he here, urging me to finish what he could not, whispering to me: Do it right, do it right? Or ... am I influenced by something else, some other spiritual presence?

I can only conclude that if not he, then the ragthorn is my guide. This would beg the question: Why? Why would the thorn wish me to find the clues to its secret power over life and death, its unnatural, no, *supernatural,* force? Unless – and my heart races at the thought – *unless I am its chosen disciple!* Gilgamesh was chosen. No doubt others after him, with Alexander the last. It is possible to fail. Of course it is possible to fail. But I intend to understand, thoroughly, what is expected of me, and succeed where Alexander did not.

A low mist, thick and blunt-nosed, winds through the valley like a soft sentient beast, sniffing amongst the mosses and rocks and leaving damp crags and stunted hawthorns dripping with moisture. Its restlessness finds its way into my spirit. I find writing difficult. There is a feeling on the land of a permanent, mist-ridden dusk. I pace the house, constantly going outside to stare at the ragthorn, perched like some black-armoured mythical bird upon the crumbling dry stone wall.

Even inside the house, my eyes continually stray to the lintel, to the evidence of the tree that has it in its tendrilous grasp. My work lies scattered around the house. I am possessed by a desire to leave the place. But I cannot. I have not heard from Wilkins for months. It is a year since I have opened the Alexander folio. Something *must* happen soon. Something must happen.

April 10, 1972
THE TREE HAS GROWN. FOR the first time in years the ragthorn shows signs of growth, twig tips extending, roots inching farther across the garden, extending below the house itself. It is coming into bud, and it seems to shake, even when there are no winds.

September 17, 1972
AN ODD FRAGMENT HAS COME to light as I worked in Cambridge, searching for the Shakespearean folio owned and hidden by Lionel Pervis (the P – of the Alexander folio), who I have discovered was my great-uncle's contemporary. The fragment is a further piece of Middle English, perhaps once part of a collection of Sacred Songs.

This fragment, a faded vellum sheet pressed between the pages of a copy of the second edition of *Paradise Lost*, may once have belonged to Milton himself. Certainly, this edition of his book has annotations in his own hand, still clear despite his blindness. One is tempted to wonder whether the dying man was clutching at a truth whose greatness had only been hinted at. He had perhaps discovered this obscure and frightening stanza from a hymn and kept it as an odd symbol of hope and resurrection.

> *Quhen thow art ded and laid in layme*
> *And Raggtre rut this ribbis ar*
> *Thow art than brocht to thi lang hayme*
> *Than grett agayn warldis dignite.*

> When you are dead and buried in lime
> And the roots of the Ragthorn form your ribs
> You will then be brought back to your home
> To greet the world again with dignity.

November 22, 1974
I HAVE AT LAST FOUND a fragment of the lost folio of *Hamlet*, but not from my searches at Cambridge! It was here all the time, in the Alexander papers. One of the apparently blank sheets is not blank at all. I would not have discovered the fact but for a coincidence of dropping the sheets onto the floor and gathering them by the dim light of the hurricane lamp. The shadowy signs of word-impressions caught my attention immediately. The marks

were shallow, the merest denting of the heavy paper from the rapidly scrawled writing on the now-lost top sheet. But the impressions were enough for me to use a fine powder of lead, and a wash of light oil, to bring out the words fully.

Clearly, Alexander was privileged to hear the relevant passage from *Hamlet,* from the original prompt copy of the play, and wrote them down. Lionel Pervis would not part with the whole folio itself, and perhaps it is now destroyed.

(Even as I write these words I feel apprehensive. I am certain, those years ago, that I carefully examined these blank sheets and found nothing. I know I tested for secret ink. I *know* that. I would surely have noticed signs of overwriting.)

The fragment of *Hamlet* makes fascinating reading, and tells me much about the method: the actual means by which the process of burial and rebirth must be achieved.

Here is Alexander's account of the discovery, and his copy of the scene that some hand, later, had eliminated from the versions of Shakespeare's play that have come down to us:

> Pervis is a difficult man to talk to. His career is in ruins and he is an embittered man. He has confirmed certain thoughts, however. Added valuable insight. In summary: The most reliable text of *Hamlet* is to be found in the Second Quarto. However, no editor would dismiss entirely the text that appears in the First Folio, though scholars have proved that the

First Folio was derived from a corrupt copy of the prompt-book, used at the Globe Theatre.

Pervis's brother is a barrister of repute, in Lincoln's Inn Fields. Was present during the discovery of a hidden room in the cellars of his firm's building, which had been walled up and forgotten. A mountain of documents was discovered in that room, among them several pages of a manuscript of great interest to Shakespearean scholars. Pervis (the barrister) sent these to his brother, in order for the Shakespearean actor to assess their worth in academic terms and asked what monetary value they might have. Pervis (the actor) claimed never to have received the papers and was taken to court by his brother and, though he could not be convicted on the evidence, was widely believed to have stolen the manuscript. It ruined his life and his career.

Pervis later claimed to have been "given" a copy of the manuscript, though it is fairly certain he sold the original to a private collector who will have it now, in some safe, in Zurich. Pervis would not release the copy to anyone, but insisted that the new version must first be heard from him, playing Hamlet's ghost at the Old Vic. Victorian society was scandalised and he was refused and demands were made upon him, which sent him into retreat, somewhere in Wales. It was there I managed to track him down. He was by that time a bitter old man. He knew of me, of my reputation for scandalising the society that he believed had dealt with him meanly, and with a certain amount of gold was persuaded to part with lines of the text, including reference to the burial place of Hamlet's father, beneath the roots of an *exotic thorn tree*.

(From Act I, Scene V)

Ghost: Thus was I sleeping by a brother's hand,
Of life, of crown, of queen at once dispatched,
Cut off even in the blossoms of my sin,
Unhouseled, disappointed, unaneled.
No reck'ning made, but sent to my account
With all my imperfections on my head.
Aye, quarters to the four winds pointed right
Below the 'bracing ragthorne's needled limbs,
Yet by ironic touch my flesh immured,
Base metal traitoring this but perfect tomb.
O, horrible! O, horrible! Most horrible!
If thou has nature in thee bear it not,
Let not the royal bed of Denmark be
A couch for luxury and damned incest ...
But howsoever thou pursues this act,
Taint not thy mind, nor let thy soul contrive
Against thy mother aught – leave her to heaven,
And to those thorns that in her bosom lodge
To prick and sting her.
Fare thee well at once,
The glow-worm shows the matin to be near
And 'gins to pale his uneffectual fire.
To where my bones lie compassed.
Thus to thee
Adieu, adieu, adieu, remember me.
(The ghost vanishes)

I have read this speech fifty times now, and still the words thrill me. Since William Alexander had seen this verse, he must surely have seen the clear indications of *method*, the method of burial beneath the ragthorn's "root vault".

"Quarters to the four winds pointed right ..." The body positioned so that it formed a star, confirmed by that later line: *"where my bones lie compassed"*. Obviously not a *set* of compasses, because the angles on such instruments are variable. It has to be the four main points of the magnetic compass: north, south, east and west.

Then also that warning, not to take metal into the grave.

> *Yet by ironic touch my flesh immured,*
> *Base metal traitoring this but perfect tomb ...*

But for the metal, the tomb would have been perfect. (For the raising of the dead?) *Ironic touch.* That play on *irony* and the metal *iron.* Perhaps he had been buried in full armour, or an amulet, whatever, the metal touched his body and imprisoned it within the roots of the ragthorn. The miracle could not take place. Metal had negated the power of wood, a living substance.

I am this much closer to an understanding.

March 18, 1976
MY GREAT-UNCLE IS BURIED beneath the ragthorn. I say this without evidence of bones, or even a final letter from

the strange man himself, but I sense it as surely as I feel the tree feeds from the stone.

This afternoon, with a trusted local man called Edward Pottifer, I excavated into the hillside beyond the dry stone wall, where the valley slope begins to drop away steeply towards the stream. The ragthorn's roots have reached here too, but it soon became clear where Alexander himself had dug below the tree to make his tomb. We cleared the turf and found that he had blocked the passage with rubble, capping it with two slabs of slate. He must have had help, someone like Pottifer perhaps, because he could not have back-filled the passage himself. I suppose there is no record of his death because he knew it had to be that way. If a man took his body and buried it beneath that tree, it would have been done in the dead of night, in the utmost secrecy, for the church, the locals, and the authorities would surely have forbidden such a burial.

He knew the method, and yet I feel that he failed.

He is still there. I'm afraid to dig into the ragthorn root mass. I am afraid of what I shall find. If he failed, what did he do wrong? The question has enormous importance for me, since I have no wish to repeat his failure.

I am ill. The illness will worsen.

April 12, 1976
I HAVE BEEN STUDYING THE evidence, and the manner and nature of the burial is becoming clearer. At Cambridge, Wilkins has sought out all the different meanings of the

various key words and I am increasingly convinced that I have a firm knowledge of just *how* the body must be placed in the encompassing, protective cage of roots. The orientation of the body must be north-south, with the arms raised as in a cross to the east and west. There must be no metal upon or within it. The armour is stripped away, the weapons are removed. Metal is counter to the notion of resurrection, and thus I have left instructions that my back teeth are to be removed when I am dead.

May 1, 1976
IN PREPARATION FOR THAT TIME when it comes, I have now – with the help of Pottifer – dug a passage several feet long into the side of the hill, below the ragthorn. I have finally taken the same route as that followed by William Alexander, but a hundred years has compacted the earth well, and it is no easy task. That we are on the right track is confirmed only by the mixture of slate that appears in the soil, and the fact that the thorn *allows* our excavation to continue in this direction. We press on, striking up, away from the bedrock. We did attempt other passages at first, but with every foot in the *wrong* direction there was a battle to be made with the protecting thorny roots. They snagged at our flesh and pulled at our hair, until we had to abandon those first diggings. The tree knows where it wants to put me.

May 3, 1976

I HAVE FOUND THE REMAINS of an infant! Thank God Pottifer was not with me at the time, for it would have shaken him badly. There is a reference in the passage from Gilgamesh: *"and when the child was born, Utnapishtim gave it at once to Old Man Who Would Be Young, and the first berry appeared on the branches."* William Alexander planted this particular shoot or cutting of the tree and would have needed a similar offering. The thought horrifies me that some mother in a nearby village, or some passing gypsy family, lost their newborn child one Victorian night.

May 10, 1976

POTTIFER HAS MADE THE BREAKTHROUGH. He came scuttling out of the hole, his face black with earth, his fingers bloody from his encounters with sharp slate and wild thorns.

"Bones!" he cried. "Bones, Professor. I've found bones. Dear God in heaven, I touched one."

He stared at his hand as if it might have been tainted. I crawled into the passage and edged along to the place where he had found my great-uncle. The earth here was looser. The cage of roots was behind me and I could feel into what seemed to be a soft soil. It was possible to work my hands through and touch the dismembered bones and the ribs of the man who lay there. Every bone was wrapped around with the fibrous worm-like rootlets of the tree.

I became very disturbed. I was invading a place that should have been inviolate, and felt that I was an unwelcome intruder into this earthy domain.

My great-uncle had failed to attain resurrection. He had done something wrong and now, I swear, the tree has his soul. It had sucked his spirit from his body to strengthen itself, perhaps to extend its root system, its power over the surrounding landscape? Was this the price of failure, to become the spiritual slave of the tree? Or am I just full of wild imaginings?

Whatever, the embrace of those roots is not a loving one, but one of possession. It is a cruel grip. The tree had hung on to the ash urn of Patroclus because the bones must not be burned. It had not released the flesh of Hamlet's father because there was metal on the body. But *I* am determined to triumph.

When I touched my ancestor's skull, I drew back sharply, then probed again. There were no teeth in the jaws. The skeleton was also orientated correctly: north, south, east and west.

It was as I withdrew my probing hand from the soft-filled earth chamber that my fingers touched something cold and hard. I noted where it lay, that it was at the top of the leg, close to the spine and clutched it and drew it out.

Edward Pottifer stared at the iron ball in my hand. "That's from an old gun," he said, and at once I remembered the story of my great-uncle's skirmish in the Middle East. Yes. He had been shot and close to death.

They had operated on him in the field, but then transported him, delirious, to a hospital in Cyprus, where he recovered. He must have been under the impression that the bullet was removed from his body at that first operation. Of course, his back would have pained him at times, but old wounds do that, without iron in them. That must have been it, for he surely wouldn't have taken the chance, not after finding the method in *Hamlet*.

I did not mean to laugh. It was not disrespect, but relief. He had carried that iron ball into the grave with him. He had removed his teeth, perhaps gold-filled, but not the bullet.

I spoke carefully and succinctly to Edward Pottifer. I told him my teeth were to be removed at death. That my body was to be stripped and *no* metal, not even a cross around my neck, was to be buried with me. My body would be a cross. I marked clearly where my head was to be placed, and how my arms should be raised to the sides. "I will give you a compass. There must not be the slightest deviation."

He stared at me for a long time, his young face showing the anguish he felt. "When do you expect that might be, sir?" he asked me. I assured him that it would not be immediately, but that I was in my fifties now, and a very ill man. I told him to come every day to the house, to make sure I was still alive, and to become familiar with me, and less afraid of me. And of course, I would pay him well for his services. Work was not easy to find in the dale, and the temptations of this offer were too strong for him: I have my gravedigger, and I know he can be trusted.

December 24, 1976
AS I WRITE THIS I am experiencing a sense of profound awe. Young Wilkins is here, and he is frightened and shocked. He arrived at the cottage last night, an hour or so before I was ready to retire. I had not expected him. He had travelled from London that afternoon, and had decided not to telephone me from the station. I understand his reasons for coming without forewarning.

I wonder what it must have felt like for him to be picking through the decaying fragments of several old parchments – brought to Cambridge by Abdullah Rashid, who subsequently vanished! – separating by tweezers and pallet knife those shards of some ancient writer's records that showed any legible writing at all; how it must have felt to be sorting and searching, eyes feasting upon the forgotten words ... and then to find John the Divine himself!

The writing is fragmentary. The state of ruination of the scrolls is appalling. The Arab traders had already cut each precious document into forty pieces, thinking that by so doing they would increase forty-fold the value of their find. And they were struck by the Hand of Calamity as surely, as certainly, as if Jehovah himself had taken control of their fate. All of them are now imprisoned. Abdullah Rashid is now an exile (perhaps even dead?). Yet he was compelled to come to England, to seek me out ... to bring his last "gift" (he asked for nothing in return) before disappearing into the night.

I was fated to discover these parchments.

It is the last reference of the ragthorn that I shall discover. No more is needed. It is a fragment that has given me *courage*.

At last I understand my great-uncle's reference to REVELATION! He had heard of the lost passage from Revelations of St. John the Divine. Perhaps he saw them? It was enough for him too. Revelation! Triumph!

Oddly, the references to resurrection are not what has frightened Wilkins. If he is afraid it is because he feels that too many of his beliefs are being threatened. He has been sobered by the encounter. But he saw the words "thorn" and "rag" and has brought to me my final, most conclusive proof that there is indeed a lost and forgotten mechanism for the resurrection of the dead, nature's alchemy, nature's embrace, a technique that defies science. No scientist will accept the revivification of the flesh under the influence of thorn, and root, and cold clammy earth. Why should they? But it happened! It has been recorded throughout history; it had begun, perhaps, in ancient Sumeria. There have been deliberate attempts to lose, to deny the fact ... folios have been scratched out, poems obliterated, classics rewritten ... the words of the ancients have been edited dutifully, perhaps by frightened servants not of God, but of *dogma* that preaches only the resurrection of the *soul*...

Oh, the irony! Oh, the pleasure at what St. John the Divine has told me.

It was all there for us to see, all the symbols, all the truths. The wooden cross, which He himself fashioned in His carpenter's shop, ready for the moment of His thricefold death, drowned, stabbed, and hanged on the tree.

The Crown of Thorns, His mastery over the forest.

The immortal wood, the tree of life, the regenerating forest – of course it can shelter and protect the mortal flesh. There is in the tree a symbol, a reality too powerful for monks with quill pens to dare to fight, to challenge. So they cut it out, they *excised* it. In this way cutting out the soul of John, they cut out the heart from the past.

"He that dies by the wood shall live by the wood."

Perhaps I have the original copy of the parchment, the *only* copy remaining? It was found in a jar, in the hills of Turkestan, and had come into the possession of Abdullah ... and had done so because it was *meant* to find its way into my hands.

For now I shall record in the journal only part of what St. John said. It is from Chapter 10 of the Revelations. It might have preceded verse 3. It is my great hope. It has confirmed my faith in the rightness of what I shall achieve. A miracle occurred in the house of Lazarus.

> *And I looked into the Light, and Lo, I saw Him command a thorn tree to spring from the roof of the house of Lazarus. And the tree had seven branches and on each branch there*

were seven times seven thorns. And below the house seven roots formed a cradle around the dead man, and raised him up so that again his face was in the light.

So cometh the power of the Lord into all living things.

And again He cried: That ye might rise anew and laugh in the face of Death, and blow the dust from thy lungs in the eyes of Death, so that ye can look on Hell's face and scorn the fires and rage upon the flames and rise thee up.

And Lo, I saw how the thorn withered and died and the Angel of the Lord flew from its dust.

And He cried out in the voice of the Immortal King:

The Lord is in all things and He is in the One Tree. He that dies by the wood shall live by the wood. He that dies by the thorn shall live again by the thorn.

April 15, 1978

POTTIFER WAS HERE. I SENT him to the tree, to begin to clear the chamber. The pain in my chest is greater than I can bear sometimes. I must refuse the sensible remedy of moving to London, to be closer to the hospital that can relieve such things, and extend my life, even though they cannot cure me.

Pottifer is very calm. We have kept the secret from the village and not even his family knows. He has managed to clear the root chamber whilst keeping the failed bones of my ancestor undisturbed below a thin layer of soil. As long as I am within that quivering cage of thorns I shall succeed. I shall live again.

There is a great danger, however. I believe now that the tree took William Alexander, body and soul, for its own. Perhaps that is its exacted compensation for the failure of its disciples, to possess *all* that remains, not just the flesh, but the spirit also?

I *know* I have it right, and I can depend on Pottifer, completely, just as my great-uncle must have depended on such a man. Pottifer is devoted to me, and obeys me implicitly.

September 11, 1978 (extract)
THE MOMENT IS VERY CLOSE. I have now acquired a set of dental pincers with which to perform the final part of the ritual. Pottifer has seen into my mouth and knows which teeth to pull.

September 20, 1978
POTTIFER IS WITH ME. I am certainly going. How vigorously the body clings to life, even when the mind is urging it to relax in peace. There is no longer any pain. Perhaps the closeness of death banishes such mortal agonies. I can hardly move, and writing is now an effort of will. This will be the final entry in my journal. Pottifer is very sad. I admire him. I have come to like him very much. His great concern is to get my body into the chamber before the *rigor* of death stiffens my limbs. I have told him to relax. He has plenty of time. Even so, he need wait only

a few hours for the *rigor* to pass. I have thought of everything. I have missed no point, no subtlety. When I am gone, Pottifer will end this journal and wait for one year and one day before returning to Scarfell Cottage. These papers, I am sure, will not be there. They will be in my own hands. If they *are* still in evidence, Pottifer is to send them to young Wilkins, but I am absolutely certain that I will be here to decide their fate, just as I have decided my own.

Adieu, or rather *au revoir*.

September 21
THIS IS POTTIFER. THE DOCTER told me to rite this when he was gone. I berried him as he told me to, and no dificulties. He said there must be no mistakes and spoke of the tree saying it sucked men dry of there souls who make mistakes. His last words to me were Pottifer I must face Hell and look on its face like Saint John tells. He seemed very fearfull. I give him a kiss and said a prayre. He shouted out in pain. You do not understand I must first look on Hells face he shouted you must berry me face down.

I said to him, you are a good man docter, and you shall *not* face Hell. You shall face Heaven as you diserve. Saint John does not need your penance. Do not be fearful of Hell. You are to good and if you come back I shall be your good friend and welcome you straight.

Then he died. His fists were clenched.

He is in the earth now and all that I have is his teeth, God bless him. I wanted to put a cross but the thorns have grown to much and there is green on tree and I do not like to medle to much since there is more growth and very fast. No one has seen the tree so green and florished for a long wile not since that time in the last centry so the tales go.

P.S.

THIS IS POTTIFER AGEN. I have got some thing more to say. Some thing odd has hapened. It is more than one year and one day. The docter is still in the ground. I was in the pub and a man came in and asked for a drink. He said he was the royal poet. I think he said his name was John Betcherman. He had been walking near Scarfell and had seen the tree. He had felt some thing very strange about the place he said. A strong vision of death. Someone screaming. He was upset. He asked about the cottage but I said nothing. He wrote a poem down and left it on the table. He said there I have exercised this terrible place and you have this and be done with it. Then he left. Here is the poem. It makes me feel sad to read it.

> *On a hill in highland regions*
> *Stands an aged, thorny tree*
> *Roots that riot, run in legions*
> *Through the scattered scrub and scree:*
> *Boughs that lap and lock and lace*
> *Choke the sunlight from that place.*

Deep below its tangled traces
Rots the corpse of one unknown
Gripped by roots whose gnarled embraces
Crush the skull and crack the bone.
Needled fingers clutch the crown
Late, too late to turn face down.

~

THERE WERE THESE TWO BRITISH writers, one lived in the country, the other in the city. The country writer loved to visit the city and partake of brandy and Greek kebabs in the local hostelry. The city writer liked to visit the country and guzzle ale and barbecued steak under the apple trees. The two writers needed an excuse for these indulgences, and so they invented one, and this excuse was called "collaborating on a story" ... It soon emerged that the story was to be about a legendary tree, which they both vaguely recalled from the tales their grandfathers used to tell them of mystery and myth. Soon they were delving with suppressed excitement into old documents at the British Museum and began to come up with some frightening discoveries.

The first of these finds was in studying the original text, in Anglo-Saxon, of the Old English poem "The Dream of the Rood". The marrying of the "tree" (crucifixion cross) and the "thorn" (a runic character) was too elaborately regular to be an accident of metre or alliterative language. Other discoveries followed, and the story gradually surfaced, like a dark secret from its burial mound.

The tall, hairy-faced writer, his eyes shining in the near darkness of the British Museum at five o'clock on a winter's evening, said, "We've got something here, mate." The short, clean-shaven writer, his hands full of trembling documents, answered with true English understatement, "You're not wrong, mate." So between them they began writing the history of the terrible "ragthorn tree".

Then again, they could have invented the whole thing, like these bloody storytellers do. As their old grandfathers used to say, "Why spoil a good story by sticking to the truth?"

Robert Holdstock
Garry Kilworth

THE FABULOUS BEAST

Garry Kilworth

To S.H.

(The following passages have been taken from a journal found in a fireproof box in the smouldering ruins of Chalkdown Farm. I trust you to assess their worth, both as a possible record of actual events and of their financial value if the contents are proven to be factual. I would be grateful for your complete discretion on this matter until we have established those two points. How you proceed to reach a conclusion I have no idea, but I have been told you are the best person to approach on matters of this kind. I shall be in London until the end of the year and await with anticipation your findings.)

Yours, R.L.S.

~

I HAVE A ROOM HERE in Amman in Khalid Ibn Al Walid Street (few of the road names consist of only single words) overlooking a market. The noise is bad but the privacy good. My Palestinian landlord is a discreet individual who knows of my interest in the Dead Sea scrolls and is of the opinion that those who sold the scrolls on the black market ought to have important parts of their anatomy removed and displayed for the benefit of the populace. He is a Christian but believes the scrolls should have remained in Jordanian hands, in the country where they were discovered.

At the time the scrolls were found at Qumran, on the north west shore of the Dead Sea, modern Jordan was only a few months old, having been governed by the British since they had wrested it in 1922 from the Ottoman Empire. The Turks had administered it as part of Syria; the British called it Transjordan. In the winter of 1946/47 it became the independent Hashemite Kingdom of Jordan under the rule of King Hussein.

A Bedu shepherd boy named romantically Muhammad-the-Wolf found the scrolls in a cave after one of his flock went missing. The archaeological treasures were in sealed earthenware jars, a total of seven, wrapped in linen. The scandal that followed the discovery, of marketing the scrolls, procrastination, incompetence, secrecy, and a host of other unfortunate occurrences, is now part of history. Those few scrolls which did remain in Jordan had been placed at my disposal due to the influence of an acquaintance of Colonel Douglass. I was in Amman to study *The War Scroll* – to search for references for a book Douglass was writing. I had found nothing really to excite him in this scroll, though the passages where *the sons of light* fought with *the sons of darkness* might hold some interest. I had also however obtained a single fragment of a leather scroll found later in one of the nine further caves – Cave 7 in fact – on which there was a reference to a *strange and marvellous beast*. This was the kind of information Colonel Douglass was desperate to obtain, thin though it appeared to me.

Yesterday evening, while I was studying this fragment which, like all those in found in Cave 7 was in Greek, not Hebrew or Aramaic, there was a sharp knock on the door. I pulled back the bolt, fully expecting to see my landlord only to find a stranger confronting me.

The man stepped smartly into the room without being invited and shut the door quickly behind him.

"*Mr* David Wilkins? My name is Abdulla Rashid," he said in a low tone, "and I am known to your master, Colonel Douglass."

"You are mistaken," I said.

He had been in the process of undoing a hessian sack and he gave a little cry and started to re-tie the bag.

"You are not Mr Wilkins?"

"I am David Wilkins," I replied, to put him at his ease, "but Colonel Douglass is not my master, nor anything like it – I'm a freelance researcher, not a slave."

He smiled at this, revealing several gold teeth "Ah-ha, you joke with me, Mr Wilkins. But I have here in this bag something you will not laugh at. I have found another amphora at the Pharos site …"

Something dawned in my memory. "Ahhh, you're the man Colonel Douglass met in Egypt! I remember he told me you had found several ancient parchments for him."

Rashid gave a little bow and smiled again.

He began undoing the sack. "What I have here for you, this time, are two parchments — no, not parchments, *hides* - from the ancient time of Jesus Christ — such as those you have come to see in Jordan."

"You mean *scrolls?*" I said, excitedly.

He shrugged. "I think so. These are not made of paper or bronze, like some, but of animal skin — you know? The language is Aramaic — I have looked at it myself. The writer is talking of a strange animal that roamed the Earth before we came here — before men walked in the world."

"You understand Aramaic?"

"And Hebrew, and Ancient Greek — what, you think I am ignorant? why do you think I peddle in such things? — because I know the worth of my goods? If I were a goatherd, I would give them to you for nothing, but unfortunately for you," he grinned gold at me again. "I am a learned man."

"Can you leave them with me until tomorrow morning? I'll meet you at the coffee shop on the corner of the market. If the scrolls are any good to me, I'll pay you then — if not, you can have your goods back."

"You think I can trust you?" he asked, but with a trace of humour in his voice.

"You most certainly can. Colonel Douglass will be my bond – you know that."

He nodded and handed over the sack. "Treat my goods well, until they are yours, then you may burn them for all I care."

With that he left. I bolted the door behind him.

FEVERISHLY I OPENED THE SACK and took out the two scrolls, wrapped in linen. I carefully removed the first one from its protective cover. Under the dim light of a twenty-five watt bulb I attempted to decipher the Aramaic script. The contents appeared to be a list, of arms and men, and I wondered if what I had here was simply another War Scroll, a kind of quartermaster's inventory.

The second scroll, which I laid carefully alongside the first on the wooden table top, disappointingly seemed to be a continuation of the first, though I did find a reference to "the creature which we call The Mother" which seemed to me to be promising.

While I stared at the second scroll, my eyes sore from working under such poor light, something happened to make me jerk backwards and stare in disbelief. It seemed to me that the two scrolls had moved closer together, independently, as if attracted to each other magnetically.

Indeed, I subsequently only managed to keep them separated by some effort. It seemed as if the edges were melding together, melting into one another, as if made of soft hot wax.

Unsurprisingly, this strange phenomenon interested me more than the texts on the hides. I studied the edges of the scrolls and found their rippling hems locked easily together like pieces of a jigsaw. From their markings they appeared to be two halves of one animal skin — possibly a goatskin, or gazelle hide — which had been cut right down the middle into two sections.

I placed the two edges together again. Once more they merged at the edges. It was astonishing. This time I left the two parts to join thoroughly, seeing no harm in allowing their union. Within in an hour it was impossible to part them without the use of a sharp implement.

This incredible curiosity excited me a great deal and I knew now that Rashid had made a definite sale, whatever his price.

I HAVE ACQUIRED THREE MORE pieces of the strange hide. One was a covering for a scabbard which sheathed an antique Oriental sword belonging to the Museum of Macau. I recognised the hide by the unique markings, which revealed a close relationship with the two (now one) piece I already own. Chinese pirates obtained it for me while it was on its way across the mouth of the Pearl River to Hong Kong airport, destined for an exhibition in Paris. The second, a strip, was a large bookmark in a sacred volume owned by Buddhist priests in Burma. And finally, the best and largest, there was a Zulu war shield, said to belong to Shaka himself and used to decorate the gate to his kraal.

The extraordinary markings – their singularity, for in all my years of research in and around the museums of the world I have never come across such hide – lead me to believe that they belonged to a creature which has been lost to human knowledge. A marvellous beast of some kind, like the sabre-toothed tiger, or the mammoth, yet even more distinct, more rare than either of those prehistoric creatures. If I can obtain more pieces – and I certainly intend to try – I shall endeavour to recreate the original shape. I am helped in this by the ability of the material to join with itself at the appropriate positions.

COLONEL DOUGLASS IS DEAD. IN a way I am relieved. My research for him was getting in the way of my true work: to restore the beast. Since discovering the first two skins, which were luckily part of the same document, I have gradually been gathering more of the whole hide. Most of the sections – though certainly not all – have been used to record sacred works. (Not surprising considering the nature of the pelt and the creature from which it came.) Among those gathered, stolen, purchased and permanently borrowed, are:

AN ANCIENT AND SACRED NATIVE American (Pawnee) drumskin.

A TIBETAN RELIGIOUS BANNER, SUPPOSEDLY carried by those priests guarding the Dalai Lama, when he was taken to India after the Chinese invaded Tibet. It was stolen by badmashes on one of the mountain passes and sold on by them to a curio collector in New York.

THREE *KHANA* OR SECTIONS OF a Mongol-Kalmuck ceremonial yurt.

A CLOAK USED IN THE rituals of the two Afghanistan Pushtun tribal divisions – the Ghilzai and the Durrani. (These two groups were forever fighting over ownership of the garment.)

BOOK COVERS FOR A UNIFORM edition of the works of Aleister Crowley, including his writings on Thelema and the Hermetic Order of the Golden Dawn. (It was in one of these books that I found my first insight as to the original owner of the whole hide. Crowley writes of a *unique* fabulous creature which roamed the earth in prehistoric times, from whose womb sprang other forms of life.)

SEVERAL OF THE PIECES OF the precious hide have come into my possession through diligent research. There are medieval stories of knights on quests: I have been on many quests in search of many grails. Fortunately I have no concerns about money. To put it bluntly, since Colonel Douglass died and made me his benefactor I am a rich man. Inherited wealth. I can think of no better purpose for my money than using it to restore a creature previously lost to natural history. In any case, it is an investment. The colonel stipulated in his will that his fortune should only go to me if I continued with his work: well, I believe I am continuing with his obsession. Oh, yes, it has also become an obsession with me now. When I have gone as far as I can go with it, I am sure the museums of the world will be bidding for possession of it. What dreams I have in that recreation! My head is spinning with the wonder of it all. I am so lucky. So very lucky. To have found – albeit by accident – a previously unknown extinct creature which will ensure my immortality in the world. I will be up there with the Leonardo de Vincis, the Isaac Newtons. I will be the man who found and recognised an unknown fabulous beast.

DESPITE ITS AGE THE THATCHED cottage in Wiltshire is proving an ideal central location for the pursuit of fragments of the beast's skin and their painstaking and oddly dangerous re-assembly. Not far from the cottage itself is a huge barn, out of time with the dwelling, but standing on secluded land common to both. As tenant of the cottage I am entitled to use of the barn. It is a massive wooden structure, criss-crossed with beams, at one time used not only to store hay, but also to house cattle during the winter on two storeys. There is a kind of drawbridge arrangement which drops from the first floor of the building to the ground which once allowed the animals a sloping run up to the top stalls. When the beast is ready to enter the world, it will be by this ramp.

Colonel Douglass himself was too obsessed with his personal goal to bother with the barn, but it is the perfect place to store and examine fragments of the beast as I uncover them. When I first discovered the barn the structure was sound: the cross members, purlins and yoke braces are all of solid oak, as strong now as when they were in Elizabethan times. Some of the jack rafters needed attention and the planking on the walls had grown flimsy, but my handyman William Enifer is a fair carpenter and is up to renovating any rotten struts. The illumination is good, through the skylight windows which William fitted and is almost of an artist's studio quality: a soft, dusty light, falls obliquely on the subject from both sides. Like most of the older buildings which look out over the moors, there is a window in the shape of a crucifix under the gables at the east end. A lamp within this window, when lit, helps to comfort and guide lost souls on the wasteland at night.

Much to William's chagrin I no longer light the lamp within the cross, since I want no strangers entering the barn, lost or otherwise.

EVEN AS I ACQUIRE MY pieces, my strips, my sheets of hide, the great three-dimensional jigsaw begins to take shape in the the barn. I ponder on Crowley's sentence, especially on that word, *unique*. He surely could not have meant there was only *one* beast? A single creature with no means of reproducing its own kind? That would make it a direct creation of God or nature, depending on your beliefs. An Adam without an Eve. Or perhaps – since Crowley seems to believe the beast produces *other* creatures, an Eve without an Adam. Yet – and the thought makes my heart pound in my chest with excitement – perhaps it could be so? If it were true, what would be the creature's lifespan? A hundred years? A thousand? Ten thousand? Or even – forever? The pieces join, as if life were still in them. Perhaps the creature has not died at all, its many parts merely scattered too widely for it to show signs of life?

THIS IS UNBELIEVABLY WONDERFUL! I do not have to find *all* the pieces to the complete hide. Where there are gaps it grows between them. The area around these spaces has to be complete, but a hole the size of a broad-brimmed hat simply fills itself overnight. Even more astonishing it is becoming a solid entity, not an empty skin which I later have to stuff. The beast constructs its own shape not only from without but now also from within. It continues to grow like a fungus feeding on its own remains, filling the empty sac.

Bones have formed within, and flesh around those bones. *Behold, the marvellous* an old poem begins. I now behold it. I don't know *how* it's happening. It's not magic, I know that much. I don't believe in magic. It has some sort of science behind it – a tree-grafting, flesh-grafting science – which has been lost to, or was never ever discovered by humankind. Once the hide was on its way to completion some sort of chemistry took over, began to produce secretions which encouraged the growth and reproduced the cells from what it already had. There is a racial memory there amongst those cells, which has been unlocked, and is now rampant. The beast forms itself by the hour, the day, the month. It will be whole before long.

I DECIDED TO SHOW MY beast to William this morning. I took him into the barn, up the wooden stairs where he stopped dead at the top, stunned by the sight which he beheld in the shafts of dusty sunlight coming through the windows.

It is a magnificent, enormous creature. No animal beauty, but awesome in its length and girth. At least twice the size of an elephant and, if I were to liken its shape to another animal form, I would say it resembles an Artic musk ox, though the hair is not quite so shaggy, nor so long as on that shambling herbivore. It has grown horns: marvellous high curving horns that start by going in, towards its massive skull, then sweeping outwards, slimming elegantly to finely-pointed tips. They grow with some kind of indigo pattern which appears to be etched in their surfaces. These resemble tattoos, on much the same design as the markings on the actual hide: centripetals, swirls, mazes. There are great hooves, these not cleft, on the end of its legs, and a broad, bushy tail trails the dust on the floor of the barn like a bridal train.

As Crowley has written, it is of the female gender.

William viewed my creation with awe in his eyes.

"Oh, Lord save us," said William, crossing himself. "I'm lost what to say, sir."

"Say nothing, William," I murmured. "Just drink in the sight of a creature seen by no human before you and me. When this beast roamed the earth Man was just a twinkle in God's eye."

"What are you goin' to do with 'im?"

"I'm not sure yet."

William looked me directly. "Why show it to me, sir?"

This was a good question and one to which I had no satisfactory answer. I suppose I wanted a reaction, even from someone like William; some praise possibly, for my work to date; a boost to the ego. I had performed a miracle and I needed to be supported in my sense of achievement. There was no other living person I could show the beast to, except William, whose simple discretion I knew I could rely upon. Colonel Douglass had trusted William completely, because he was of that eremite breed which holds things close, does not gossip to friends let alone strangers, and guards his secrets more jealously than the sphinx does hers.

"I thought you might like to see it. You must have wondered what I was up to in here. I wanted to satisfy your curiosity on that score."

William gazed at the beast, his critical Wiltshire yeoman's eye roving over the creature as it might do over some strange giant which had stumbled off the Salisbury Plain. He shook his head, wonderingly.

"*What* is it?" he asked at last.

"Honestly? I don't know."

"You're not having a joke a with me, are you?" He looked up and around, into the rafters and towards the back of the barn. "You got some sort of mechanics? Bellows and what not? Some sort of wind pump, eh? You made it up, didn't you?"

I was confused. "You mean did I construct it myself? A fake? No, no. This is an actual creature which once lived on our planet. It is destined for some museum, I suppose."

"Museum?" retorted William, edging back down the stairs. "Zoo, more like. It's bloody breathin'. That bugger's *alive*."

A chill went through me. I turned and stared hard at the beast. As I did so, it slowly lifted its great head and looked at me with clear hazel eyes.

THANKFULLY WILLIAM HAD THE GOOD sense not to rush out and blurt the discovery to the first person he might meet on the road. He did run away, but only as for as the nearest public house, The White Horse. There he quietly downed several pints of beer, slept the night in ditch, and returned to the cottage the following morning. He was still in a state of shock, but I managed to sit him down in a warm kitchen and put several mugs of coffee into him. All the while I explained to him that he and I were special human beings, chosen by some higher entity to witness the rebirth of an extinct creature.

"Who knows the secret of life?" I said to him, as I plied him with coffee. "Life as we know it simply sprang from the Earth in the beginning of the prehistory of the world and though no such similar scientific miracle has occurred since, there is no reason why such a thing can't repeat itself ..."

I was making it up as I went along, trying to persuade this pragmatic man that such a thing was not supernatural, but simply the regeneration of a natural episode in the history of mother earth. In the end, so long as I could allay his superstitious suspicion that witchcraft was involved, that it was simply an unusual and rare kind of science that was responsible, a science that was of course sanctioned by God, he seemed willing to remain as the handyman at the cottage. My work, he told me, was nothing to do with him. He was a *practical* man, with not much learning, he told me. He didn't hold with woodland magic nor any of that wayland smithy stuff, but if I said it was a natural thing, though not usual these days, then he would try not to make a fuss.

But I could see he was still not totally convinced, so I continued my gentle argument.

"There are patients in hospitals," I said, "who have died on the operating table and they have been brought back to life with by administering a bolt of electricity to their hearts.

You must have heard about things like that?" I followed this with an outright lie. "And you know, in Siberia mammoths – you know what they are? yes of course you do – well, mammoths have been found frozen whole in tombs of ice. They have been encased and preserved there since prehistory. Yet, when thawed out and treated with – with electricity – their hearts begin to beat again ..."

"There's much in the world I'm not good at understandin'," he said, "and one of them's scientific things. Someone once tried to tell me how electric works and it seemed like magic to me."

"Exactly, William. No one alive really understands electricity, but we know it's there and we know it's natural. Who's to say our creature out there in the barn did not experience a bolt of electricity during that lightning storm we had the other night? Yes, that must have been it. That wild storm that came off Salisbury Plain? You remember, William. There's our answer, eh?"

In the end, I had William in the palm of my hand.

So, the beast is alive. How that has occurred is indeed an unsolvable mystery to me, but something in the original nature of the hides contained the secret of regeneration of life. No wonder indeed that those hides had been venerated by holy men since the beginning of history. No wonder that they had been used as parchment for sacred scripts. Priests and shamans had recognised in them something unique and wonderful. Here was a new and marvellous discovery, my discovery, and a huge wave of elation went through me as I studied the beast in the mellow light from the barn's dirty windows.

SHE IS HUGE, BUT DOCILE and bovine looking. Her coat is now covered in symbols – the indigo tattoos of which I wrote earlier – and it would seem they are her camouflage. They look strangely like an enigmatic alphabet of some kind, though this might be just my imagination working overtime. Her fodder is hay and she will eat fresh grass if allowed to roam in a meadow. I am still at a loss to know what to do next. Whom should I contact? What will happen to her when I do? I feel a strong possessiveness towards my beast. Why should I hand her over to others to do with as they wish? Would I be believed if I told the story of her creation or would people think me mad? I have no doubt they would be intrigued by this creature which appears to be unique, but would they believe she was given life by my hands? I very much doubt it. They will invent stories of me finding her alive on the plain and proclaim her origin to be an unsolvable mystery. If the worst comes to the worst, they might even put her in a zoo, or some freak circus for the "public benefit"!

I listen to her slow, laboured breathing, her munching of the hay, and I'm left in this quandary as to how I'm going to launch her into the world. In the meantime we have begun to allow her out to pasture. She is so camouflaged by her indigo markings as to be almost invisible from a distance. Certainly one has to be within fifty yards of her to make out any sort of realistic shape.

She is able to roam over an area of the plain closely watched by one of us. We discourage the odd trespassing rambler and keep a keen eye for any legal army personnel. A vast area of Salisbury Plain has been the property of the Ministry of Defence for many a long year and is used for army exercises and manoeuvres. In truth the farm is just inside the border of MOD property, but farms such as mine are permitted to continue their livelihood and ownership of private land that has been theirs for centuries on the understanding that the ministry has rights of access on occasion. Thankfully neither William nor I have ever seen a tank nor unit of swaddies anywhere near the farm.

I have purchased rifles for William and myself so that we might protect her from any harmful animals, such as foxes or wild dogs. William asked whether he was to fire on any humans that approached our creature. I told him it was inadvisable, even though we were protecting our rights, but I voiced it in such a way as to give him the idea that the law would understand it if we found it a necessary action to take. William grew up with firearms – shotguns to fill the pot and rifles to rid the land of rooks – and is an excellent marksman. I have not had such an upbringing but my own weapon is of the best quality, and with telescopic sights is easy to handle, aim and fire with accuracy.

STAGGERING! INCREDIBLE!

It was William who three weeks ago discovered that the beast had given birth to a creature, as prophesised by

Crowley. But what an amazing creature! Since then there have been one or two more births, as astonishing as the first. My plain-thinking William is again upset and shaken of course by the wild strangeness of this turn of events. One would be. But I shall bring him round to my way of thinking, which is that this is a link that has been missing from Creation since Man came into the world.

The first birth was a half-grown unicorn, its symbolic single horn unmistakable, though this appendage was pliable at first and only hardened later. There followed a griffin, then a fox-like creature but clearly one we would term "mythical", followed by a senmurv and a winged lion known as a lamassu. All are fabled creatures that over the centuries have formed part of our different national cultures, but which most today regard as fictional. We all know the red dragon, and the green, both of which have been adopted as symbols of national pride. However, no one in today's civilised world recognises the dragon as a real creature, living or extinct, and simply accepts that it was an invention of Man's vivid creativity.

A small cluster of "mythological" animals have been given birth. All of these creatures are, it seems, sexless. They appear to have no means of reproducing themselves, which was obviously why there was a need for a "mother" creature to provide the birthing function. The beast, the fabulous being which I have recreated, is the mother of those legendary creatures.

William and I corralled our collection of fabled beasts in a large spreading outhouse once used for housing pigs, the individual stalls perfect for the job. Our minds were reeling with possibilities. Even William, in his state of ignorance, was now aware that we had the makings of everlasting fame and fortune in our hands. I needed time and space to think, it being crucial to make the right decision on how to present this discovery to the world. It is so big, so earth-shattering in its revelation, I know that even so-called incorrupt governments would have no hesitation in ignoring laws regarding ownership. I do not want my discovery taken out of my hands immediately I make it known to the world, which is what will happen if I do not take firm, prior steps to protect my proprietorial rights. I am uncertain how to do this, but I do not intend to proceed without establishing some sort of defence.

As an aside, with each new birth the mother beast sloughs her skin. This shedding is not of the thickness of the original hides which I had fitted together to give life to my beast, but is nevertheless strong enough to serve as a fabric. I have made shirts out of the skins for William and myself to wear when we are out with the mother beast as she roams her pastures. I have also fashioned blankets for our horses. These provide camouflage and make us as invisible as she is herself on the rugged Wiltshire landscape.

We are her outriders, ever watchful and jealous of her safety, our rifles always loaded and cocked ready for use. I have reached the point where I would have no hesitation in preventing anyone who tries to harm her. I am her protector. She is more precious to me, to the world, than any other living creature. There is not one other animal alive, including man or woman, who is more valuable to the heritage of our planet. A heritage lost until my discovery.

THE SHIRTS HAVE BECOME IMPOSSIBLE to remove. They first stuck to our bodies, then melded, and now they form a new skin over the old. I joke with William that we have become Maori warriors, but he is quite traumatised by this state of affairs and scrubs himself with a floor brush incessantly, trying to remove the indigo markings. For myself I am happy with this new situation. I feel it brings me closer to the mother beast and her offspring, as if they are my siblings, the unicorn, the griffin, the wonderful dragon. I feel refreshed in my mind and am experiencing a new beginning to my life. The rest of the world may rush by and headlong into new forms of music, pastimes and fashion, but we here in our hidden corner of Wiltshire are happy to wait for the right moment to reveal to humankind a new page in the history of our planet.

DISASTER.

I woke just three hours ago, at 2 o'clock in the morning, with William shaking me by the shoulder.

"Fire!" he yelled at me. "Fire! Fire!"

Roused from a deep sleep I was befuddled and all I could see by the strange flickering light coming through my window was a mad-eyed William. His voice was shrill and he appeared almost demented. I sat up quickly and shook my head, trying to clear it sufficiently to listen to his shouts.

"The piggery, sir! It's on fire."

The piggery? I leapt out of bed and pulled on a pair of trousers. Then we both rushed outside and William pointed, unnecessarily. Indeed, the old pig sties were blazing, the flames reaching thirty feet in the air. There was the stink of burning hair and flesh, which made me gag on my breath. The heat was tremendous as the red and yellow inferno swallowed the blackness above it and oxygen rushed in from beneath to further fuel the disaster. Thankfully the screams of the trapped residents ceased after a very short while.

"Did you manage to save any?" I cried, hopefully. "The creatures, are any still alive?"

William shook his head as we both stared at the conflagration. Nothing inside that building was going to escape. The lower part, perhaps reaching three feet from the ground, was brick, but the upper walls and roof were timber. Inside the piggery there had been heaps of hay and straw everywhere. Once a fire started in there, it would have spread very quickly. I now see how inflammable the building was, but now is too late. I should have thought about it earlier, though if I am honest with myself I have not been attentive to ordinary matters lately, being on a higher plane with my dreams of triumph.

"William," I said, "how did it start? Did you drop the hurricane lamp?"

"No – no, sir. I was in with Her Majesty," he answered, pointing to the old barn, "but then there's more bad news there, eh?"

The hairs on the nape of my neck rose. "What bad news?"

"She's gone. Busted out. Ran off somewhere."

"What?"

"Not my fault," cried William, backing away from me. "She just lit out, when the fire started and them animals started wailin'."

I ran over to the barn, but it was dark inside and I had no torch or lamp with me. I fetched a torch and then returned to inspect the interior. The beast had indeed broken out, through the back wall of the barn. The planks there, old and somewhat rotten, had been shattered leaving a huge hole. I gathered my thoughts. This was a terrible occurrence, but not a catastrophe. Once we had saddled the horses, we would probably soon overtake the mother beast and persuade her to return, as we always did when she was put out to pasture. No doubt she would be highly strung after the night's events, but with calm handling I thought we would get her home safely.

It was then I heard a sound, a low moan. I looked at her straw bedding and shining my torch I saw a naked form there, slick with afterbirth. It was the latest arrival from her anomalous womb, obviously abandoned by the mother when she panicked and crashed through the wall of the barn and out into a dark night on the plain. I stared at the creature caught in my torchlight. It blinked and then did something that chilled me to the bone, a signal that this new "mythical" creature was more than just another fabled animal. There was astuteness there and other major differences. I knew for one thing for absolute certainty, that though it might have originally been born androgynous, somewhere in its history on the Earth it had developed the means to procreate.

"Oh my God," I whispered.

I stood staring down at this fresh birth in horror. The implications raced through my mind as the creature reached out to touch me with one extended limb. William was just coming through the barn doorway carrying rifles and saying, "Horses are saddled and ready, sir." He stepped up beside me and looked down at the thing lying in the straw.

William let out a strangled cry, then croaked, "Lord have mercy!"

I believe his next action was instinctive rather than deliberate. The rifle shot sounded monstrously loud in my ear and I reeled backwards half-stunned by the sound. When I had gathered my wits it took me some long moments before I realised that William had shot the creature through the head. There were shards of bone and pieces of flesh flying everywhere. Despite my feelings of revulsion, I half-understood why William reacted thus.

But William was gone from my side. When I ran out of the barn he was already riding through the gateway, out onto Salisbury Plain.

He shouted over his shoulder, "We have to kill her too, Mr Wilkins. She's breedin' monsters. We have to kill her and burn her."

Then he and his horse were swallowed by the darkness.

I carried the remains of the creature William had shot to the burning piggery and threw them into the flames. The place was still blazing and hot enough to melt the iron hinges on the doors. Such a fire would soon destroy any evidence and we could return later and bury the ashes out on the plain.

Staring at the blackened carcasses of our erstwhile brood of so-called myths, I could make out certain shapes and suddenly realised what had started the fire. It must have been the small green dragon, of course, who no doubt had just discovered his special gift. The dragon would have experimented with its fiery breath, once its throat had developed its potential to blast away, thus destroying not only its siblings, but itself in the bargain.

I now had to ride out and find William, before he killed the mother beast and ... what was it he intended to do? Burn her? Had he taken inflammable liquid with him? There was plenty of it lying around. Paraffin for the lamps. Petrol for the farm machinery. I realised the urgency now.

I had to stop him destroying my chance of fame and fortune. Possibly William, who was not a stupid man, believed that if humankind were to discover we are not a natural species, but an aberrant lifeform produced by a deviant offshoot from what is regarded as normal and scientifically sound, then society would descend into chaos.

It is possible that such a revelation might eventually be welcomed as a wonderful and marvellous thing, but initially it would undoubtedly send the human race reeling from the shock of a discovery that might take decades and many violent upheavals to overcome. Old religions, cultures, beliefs and scientific philosophies would fall, new ones arise, and in that terrible mix there would be chaos and confusion, madness, terror and despair.

Yet, we had been through many shocks in our history on the Earth and have managed to overcome them without.

I swung myself into the saddle, just as a new dawn was putting her torch to the sky in the East. There is absolutely no doubt that what we had seen, that final birth of the mother before she stampeded from the barn, was mankind's close kith and kin. I saw the expression on the creature's face, clearly in the torchlight. There was no mistaking what kind of being lay in that straw at my feet.

We are the only animals on earth able to smile.

THE CHARISMA TREES

Robert Holdstock

In April 1994 I asked Rob Holdstock if he would send me a story for an anthology. Instead, on 11 June I received the following series of letters with a note from Rob saying he would contact me again in July.

David Garnett

~

Dear David,

Thank you for your note and I'm sorry to have been so slow responding. Two reasons for my distraction: first, the story I'd *planned* to show you ("Merlin's Wood") grew into a novel! And secondly, that business at Hockley Mere in Norfolk, I mentioned to you, has been taking some interesting twists and turns. I'll be getting back into Science after twenty years! Real Soon Now...

It occurs to me that the letters from the paleo-botanist who contacted me might be of interest, since they deal, as does the whole Hockley Mere "event", with a subject close to the modern SF heart.

I enclose her side of the correspondence; see what you think. In any case, I'll be in touch in July.

All the best

Rob

~

(Letters from Rebecca Knight of the Department of Botany, Cambridge University, 1992-1994)

August '92 (letter)

Dear Rob,

Thanks for the book, but especially thanks for your time and work with Phil and myself at Hockley Mere. As you've no doubt discovered, taking peat-samples from thinly wooded Norfolk Fenland is laborious, wet, tiring on the arms, and very, *very* dirty! Thank God for the Dancing Poachers pub, even if it is a gathering point for the metal-detector mafia, the bloody treasure hunters! Anyway, more to the point: our research project is not just one page further along, thanks to your efforts – it's beginning to take a whole new direction! There was something very strange and very exciting in one of the samples we took that day. I'll get to it in a moment.

For your information, since you've asked, the cores you took were two inches in diameter, went forty feet deep, reaching down through one hundred and fifty thousand years of time, more or less. We have some horrendous names for the feet and inches along that core which mark out the centuries: *Alerod* and *Windermere Interstadial* (those were the warm times); *Older* and *Younger Dryas* (the woody times); *Devensian*, *Flandrian* and *Holocene*… it goes on!

So you have sampled oak and elm wildwood at a time when only boar, bears and *beavers* hunted the magic groves. Oh yes, there were beavers at work in Norfolk a hundred thousand years ago, same style of dams, same effect on shaping the woodland around the rivers as you get in Canada.

Anyway, your core was a fine sample, and an interesting one. A "good call", as we Americans say. It has a charcoal line in the Older Dryas, followed by an inch of grassland pollen: this means that about a hundred thousand years ago the forest around Norwich burned down – a ferocious fire, by the looks of it, very localized, quite inexplicable.

The area never recovered. The climate cooled, and a sort of cold savannah took over; an open grassland scattered with stands of beech and silver birch, patches of scrub-oak and wych elm, acting as shelters to ungulates, rodents and birds of prey. This was *rich* grassland, though, and would have been grazed by many species of creature, mostly now extinct.

But most interesting of all, we've found the pollen of an equally extinct tree, a shade-tolerant ecotype of *Corylus avellana:* yes, the famous and magical British hazel, the sacred Tree of Avalon, whose nuts carry wisdom and inspiration and whose twigs can find water and make rain!

We think the ecotype must have developed and spread from a single *refugium* (that's the academic's word for the first seeding-place), which was light-starved. In other words, this tree had stamina. Or to put it another way, it had a versatile gene pool.

No: I *don't* intend to get into the debate about DNA and magic attributes! Save that for your novels!

At the risk of boring you with facts (I know you prefer your *own* facts to anyone else's), let me take a moment to walk you through some ancient echoes, just outside Norwich.

At fifty thousand years Before the Present, primary oak and elm return to what for millennia has been a rich grassland, so you can imagine the Fenland as now being a stifling, unbroken forest in three layers: a gloomy and dangerous underwood of scrub-hazel, juniper, crab-apple, maythorn and holly – below a vast sprawling canopy of oak, elm and lime, a sea of foliage that is penetrated vertically by oaks of enormous size! Grandfather trees, as they would be called in the Amazon rainforests.

But these oaks must have been *phenomenal* – nearly two hundred feet of vertical trunk, and then a vast but compact head of twisting branches, gnarled bark, leaf mass, fungal extrusions, *hollowings* and hollows in the mass. Mini-ecosystems, in other words, hovering above a broken and restless landscape of canopy and nests. (Oh yes: did I mention that we find evidence that the upper canopy was used like a *land surface,* swarming with birds and light-boned mammals, running the leaf mass above the half-light of the wildwood below, where the *big* creatures hunted?)

The core-sample you took – so much work for eight hours, so many pints that evening! – shows that during the last hundred and fifty thousand years Eastern England was covered four times by a massive wildwood. But each period of afforestation lasted no more than ten thousand years before giving way to tundra, or cold savannah.

I know you don't agree with me, but the wildwood is only an *occasional* visitor to the Earth. Because it's long-lived in human terms, and humans achieved consciousness during its last and latest visit, we think of it as *the* natural state, but the wildwood really is only one face of an Earth that is continually playing with its options. Savannah, in the heat, and tundra, in the cool, are the *real* landscape, the most cost-effective if you want to think of it in those terms. I know we all worry about the loss of forests – their beauty, their biota, their diversity, and their function as *refugia* for human populations who have become of interest to anthropologists, if that's something you can sanction. But the Earth itself seems to recognize that big forests are simply one extreme of the Life-Fluctuation norm – deserts being the other – and so what we *should* be concerned with is the *concreting* of the Earth. As long as we have fields of grass to dream in: No problem! When the fields go ... Problem!

October '92 (letter)
Dear Rob ... I've just been to a seminar on the whole Hockley Mere site, and here's some information closer to the heart of a Celtophilic, nostalgic old archaeo-culture-vulture: your core, which reached down one hundred and fifty thousand years into the past, began its journey through a vertical cut of *human* time. In the top four feet you managed to pass through the site of a Civil War skirmish, then through one of King John's camps (a small coin has been found); there are traces of a seventh-century settlement, possibly Efringdun, and a Celtic shrine, Icenian, probably associated with Boudicca or her husband, Prasitagus, and dedicated to *Mabon*. Below that, a Bronze Age cemetery with burnt offerings and obsidian beads; then a flint workshop, probably five thousand years Before Present, and finally a shell midden, almost certainly Mesolithic; a community of fisherfolk and hunters that had

lived here when the coastline of Norfolk came a lot further inland – before Cromer, before Great Yarmouth!

It's like a new excursion into *Puck of Pook's Hill*, isn't it? Downwards through time.

A foot below these echoes of Kipling's journey, the wildwood, according to its pollen record, is strong and free, reaching to the edge of the ocean itself. But six inches below that there is nothing but the signs of ice and desolation – namely sterile clays and gravels. Then, ten feet down – about twenty five thousand years ago – we find not just the wildwood again, but fire and flint!

Dear God, we think of Ancient History as Stone Age, Stonehenge, Bronze Age, Romans, Trojans, King Arthur, Robin Hood – Abba! But here, *before* the Ice Age that shaped your country as you know it, someone *lived*, made tools, burned a clearing to construct a shelter, someone *echoed the beaver*, forgotten folk shaping the land by making their refuge out of the *product* of that land.

It makes me think of the question you posed to us that final night in the pub, before you left: what did they dream of? Where are their dreams now? How do we *look* at the land in the right way to see what they might have left for us? (I'm talking forgotten folk here, not Abba ...)

November '92 (letter)
Rob ... really bad news: three evenings ago, the treasure hunters came, metal detectors in profusion. There were

five of them, possibly more, since one kept talking into a mobile phone. Typical Nighthawks – leather masks painted with bird features, army-surplus anoraks, "bovver boots" and motorcycle chains. They smashed the last two cores we'd taken – the others, fortunately, had already gone to Cambridge – and burned our tents. They said we were trespassing on a "listed site". When Phil pointed out that Hockley Mere was nothing of the sort, and he'd know because he'd done the routine search, as he did before sampling from *any* part of the land, he got two broken teeth and chain burn round his neck for his protest.

They waved a map of Britain at us – it was covered with circles, thousands of them. "Listed sites! Listed sites!" the leader chanted.

Phil did absolutely nothing physical. He just kept arguing with them. This *was* a site of archaeological interest, he roared at the leader, as the recent core-sampling would suggest. But it wasn't yet a listed site, as they must well have known. If they'd found evidence of a settlement, they should report it to the British Museum and immediately stop all metal-detecting work at the site. The only thing their map showed was archaeological sites that had been tentatively identified from the air, or by bastards like them with metal detectors, none of which had yet been officially excavated, and which in most instances were probably not even *known* officially.

Then he called them "nothing more than thieves!". "Pillagers!" he shouted. "Don't pretend differently."

That's when he got an old-fashioned police baton in the mouth, and four hundred pounds' worth of dental work. He's defiant though. This country's heritage *is* being mined for gold and silver, while "dull" things like clay plaques with scrawled writing on them, lifted from a Roman site, or boot buckles from a lost medieval village, get dumped in what the Nighthawks call Bad Find Pit.

From a stray comment heard before he was beaten up, Phil thinks Bad Find Pit is somewhere in the West York Moors, a deep ghyll of some sort, maybe even Gaping Ghyll itself. The ultimate votive-offering shaft! If that sounds flippant, I don't feel flippant. I feel sick ...

February '93 (fax)
... Do you remember the pollen of *Corylus* we found? Curiouser and curiouser ... This ecotype of the magical hazel hasn't been known for a hundred thousand years, but its DNA, in the pollen we extracted, was still intact and viable. It had been preserved in a sugar – trehalose, I think – which doesn't crystallize but instead forms a sort of *glass* – it protects molecules, even complex ones, by forming hydrogen bonds with macromolecules in place of water. That's how seeds, frogs, even some reptiles survive droughts in non-active metabolic states for decades ... but one hundred thousand years!

Apparently there are stands of *Corylus* all over the world, seeded from a Hockley Mere sample taken ten years ago. (No: I'm afraid it wasn't a new discovery after all.) It's a fast-growing tree, unlike modern hazel, and secretes organic matter in the same sugar-glass, presumably to protect itself against insect parasites – rather like resin, I suppose, although it must also *attract* creatures. I'd have thought. Do you remember visiting Wytham Woods outside Oxford? We got permission to go into the wildwood *refugium*, the few acres where they're leaving the wood unmanaged for the foreseeable future, and at one point we were both almost speechless with a sense of belonging, of beauty, of being almost in a New Age fever of closeness to nature. You wanted to hug the trees, you said. In fact you did, and got very sticky as a result. Well, that was the *Corylus* refuge. I'll try and find out more and let you know.

April '93 (letter)
… I was talking with David Bellamy at a faculty supper. Apparently on the island of Tasmania there's a swathe of forest that no lumberjack will touch, or even go near. These are hard-assed, hardwood-hating, money-seeking, western, "exploitation-vegetation" (as we call the logging companies). But they won't access Gordon Valley for love, money, or even more money! And the place is riddled with archaic *Corylus,* seeded there in '82, and now widely spread. Each *Corylus* hazel seems to create a circle of protection among the native trees, which include mahogany and the

so-called Dragon trees with their huge buttresses, a circle about four hundred yards in diameter. Bellamy said he'd heard these called Charisma Zones. To go into them was either frightening or awe-inspiring. He said he'd wanted to stay in the valley for ever and had forcibly to control what he called an emotional-overload in order to get out. But — loggers unwilling to cut the trees? Odd, to say the least.

At the same supper, listening to the same conversation, was Jack Cohen, an embryologist and science-fiction fan, I think. Do you know him? He apparently goes to sci-fi conventions and gives crazy, right-on lectures about alien biologies. He'd heard that the *Corylus avellana* seeded in Tasmania are transgenic, he's not sure how, and will arrange for me to meet Crick's assistant in the Botany department. They're playing with all manner of genetic matchmaking, as they call it, of plants.

May '93 (letter)
... It's human DNA! I can hardly believe it. The *Corylus avellana* archetypes have been "infected" with twenty gene-sequences selected from various human chromosomes (I was told which ones, but it didn't mean a lot to me), complex sequences that between them contain some, though not all — but *enough* — of the coding that combines to create the chemical and behavioral attributes we call *charisma;* the effect that some people have when they walk into a room, or talk to you — you feel drawn to them, you

feel in their shadow, but you're content, it's a form of nurture – you can't touch, but they can hold you so close. They can elicit fear, or respect, but mostly *well being* – what Americans are increasingly calling the "feel good factor", as Hollywood's own charisma cuts through the neural networks of the American psyche, leaving only sentimentality and redemption as the Theme of Life.

Charisma!

They have apparently set up small intrusions of transgenic hazel wood in fifty forest locations, each with the Group-DNA-sequences from a different charismatic individual.

The way it works is to do with the trehalose sugar-glass. The hazel tree *exudes* the charisma factor, which is protected in fluid glass and contained in molecular tubes of Buckminsterfullerene, a complex of hexagonal and pentagonal carbon rings that form together like a football but which can also link to form incredibly resistant, single-molecular thickness tubes, theoretically with no limit to their length! Each breeze in the rainforest, or temperate woodland, carries millions of these charisma packages to the foliage of the native trees, where they're absorbed through pores into the leaves, and disseminated through the sap system to individual cells. The "bucky-tubes" seem able to enter the transport systems of each plant cell through the exits in the cell membrane from the reticular system, which accumulates and pumps out cell products. Everything is in reverse, then – the human genes, linked with *Corylus avellana*'s reverse transcriptase and a so-called "seek and find" gene that targets the nuclear membrane, enters it, and allows for the stitching into the cells of the tropical hardwood (or whatever) of the viral DNA, thus allowing a gigantic and long-established hardwood to produce some of the thousands of human pheromones that can combine to create the aura of *charisma*.

By the way – you remember the *refugium* in Wytham Wood? When you hugged and kissed the trees, and called them "wonderful" and "so, so precious" and "my special luvvies"?

They were carrying the pooled DNA of five years of British Oscar winners!

September '93 (letter)
… It's not easy getting details of the charismatic *Corylus* intrusions. The original requests for DNA were made surreptitiously, but the "Charisma Set" got to hear of it, through the grapevine, in no time at all. There were *thousands* of applications to donate DNA – from politicians, actors, explorers, religious leaders, ex-hostages, painters, writers, newspaper moguls, athletes, comedians, TV presenters – it's astonishing how these people define their own charisma. How many *believe* the fake charisma of public notoriety is somehow to do with them.

Of course, money talked in its own persuasive dialect, as has politics, which is to say "blackmail".

But on the whole, the charisma – which of course is to be used to *protect* and *preserve* the woodlands – has been acquired by general agreement.

A notable success, for example, is the Clint Eastwood *Corylus* pinewood up in Montana. They call it Make-My-Day wood, and it's flourishing – mainly because no one dares go near it.

The various Geller Groves – using Uri Geller's DNA – are also having a remarkable effect. Although his spoon bending was probably a trick, his ability to stop wristwatches seems to have been genuine. But inside a Geller Grove, time doesn't just *stop,* its accumulated events *vanish,* facilitating peace meetings between enemy states that can be undertaken without the burden of history.

The hugely promoted Papwoods of Madonna have been successful too – they're so tacky and forgettable, nobody bothers with them.

Not all the *Corylus refugia* are working as well as these. The so-called Ed Kennedy copses in New England have deteriorated into shallow lakes and marshes, now used by the locals to dump their old cars. And four hundred miles from Manaus, in the Caruaru region of the Brazilian rainforest, the charismatic *Corylus* intrusion actually seemed to *encourage* the loggers and drug companies in the mindless exploitation of the local flora, causing much suffering. After several years of such abuse, however, the *Corylus* were suddenly found strangled with creeper; Thatcher wood has now been deemed a failure and will be cut down.

November '93 (scrawled letter)
... I can't bear it. I've been hysterical with rage for a week. I should have written to you at once, but sometimes I'm not strong enough to face my own despair.

Phil is in hospital, very badly hurt. He went back to Hockley Mere to take a second core, to try to establish if the charcoal feature that was discovered when you were with us was the result of human clearance by a *Sapiens* group, closely related to *Sapiens Neanderthalis,* remains of which have recently been found in abundance in Spain; it's a human group which might have spread over the fabled land bridge between Brittany and Dorset that we now know existed 80,000 years ago.

The Nighthawks must have been waiting for him, or perhaps he disturbed one of their digging operations. They threw him in the shallow mere, tied up with oiled motorcycle chains, and his skull cracked by a blow from a flint hammer, which they discarded. They'd stuck a red-kite's carcass on an ash-pole by his unconscious body, carved with – can you believe it? – early Latin. The words meant "Finding is keeping. If you spy, you die."

The arrogance, the confidence in this display of territoriality, seems to confirm what Phil always suspected – it's the millionaire collectors, the black market, the art world that is behind the Nighthawks. And our government gets a nice little earner in tax to deny it's happening, because questions aren't asked, and objects don't have to be catalogued, just so long as the monetary transaction in "sale of art" appears on the simplest of tax forms. We're so obsessed with the fine details of select committee reports, rulings, debates and decisions on our heritage, that we forget how easy it is to bribe the establishment to ignore the question of *what* is being traded, or exploited, by simply being honest about the amount of money it's being traded *for*.

Late February '94 (fax)
... You remember the woods near Hockley Mere? Three sets of men's clothes – leathers, underclothes, masks, boots, chains – plus metal detectors were found in a *Corylus* grove, strung to branches with ivy, just last week. No sign of bodies, nor signs of a struggle. And it turns out it's a Charisma wood too! But there's a certain cageyness about exactly *whose* charisma. There are five "closed files", according to Jack Cohen. Five woods, world-wide, that are "outside" the main experiment. Cambridge is completely silent on the nature – even the location – of those five. Hockley Mere has "leaked" – in part at least – but I hear already that the army is moving in.

What happened to the Nighthawks? Charisma can't *kill*, can it? It can't be the *trees* tying the clothes up ... Can it? What happened to the bodies?

Later note by post:
I just found out Phil was down there at the time, went there after discharging himself from hospital. But he wasn't around when the discovery of the discarded clothes was made, or at least no one saw him. He's not been seen for several days, in fact. I'm seriously worried, now. I'm going down to Hockley Mere to take a look – I'll call you tomorrow if all's well.

March '94 (handwritten notes on lined paper)
… The whole area around Hockley Mere has been sealed off: lakes and woods, fields and farms, the army and police are everywhere, and rangers, and paramilitaries. It's like a scene from a movie. Army trucks are in and out along the main road in a constant stream.

I caught up with Phil in the Dancing Poachers. He's managed to dig in, at Hockley, a sort of hide, close enough to the woods to see the activity at closer hand, but it's risky.

The main thing he's observed is that a stretch-limo arrives every day, driving slowly into the cluster of lorries, portacabins and tents that have been erected at the lakeside perimeter of Hockley wood. Always a cluster of people around the limo, and much activity out of sight, moving towards the woods. Who's inside, Phil hasn't seen or managed to find out yet.

Meanwhile, locals talk about the two lost kids, both in their teens, both keen on fishing in the scatter of ponds around the main lake itself. They'd gone missing three days before. Just their clothes found, neatly packaged at the woodland edge ...

March '94 (postcard)
Two army privates, who came into the Poachers' for a drink, were talking about "missing" friends. They were getting scared of the Hockley Mere duty, talking about asking for a transfer. They clammed up when Phil came and sat down nearby, but the landlady, an easy-going woman, got talking to them later. Five of their unit have gone missing, it seems, and the rest are badly affected by going *anywhere* near the trees – a dizzying sense of dislocation, void, emptiness, a feeling of being far flung, helplessly travelling towards a strong, guiding light.

March '94 (postcard, same post)
Out of body experiences? Or maybe that odd experience during near death when you seem to be going down a tunnel towards an "angelic" light? Who knows? I can't get close enough to find out. Rumor in the "scientific" world, by the way, is that the charisma is Billy Graham's, but I'm

sure Praise-The-Lord wood (the trees wave their upper branches in unison) is in the USA somewhere.

Early April '94 (fax)
... Curiouser and curiouser: a constant stream of experts on what I hear is being called "Imaginative Time" are being bused in from around the world. Many of them stop off at the Poachers'. By all accounts they are as confused by the happenings at the Charisma wood as the locals.

You'll probably know some of the writers among them: they've been brought in because of their expertise in the relationship between time and imagination: Aldiss to advise on the Jurassic; Priest on the Edwardian; Moorcock and Silverberg on the End of Time itself; Kushner and de Lint on time as it runs in the realm of Faerie; Tuttle on lost futures; Bear, Baxter, McAuley on Big Science. Several others. There are musicians – Birtwistle, Chris Dench, Laurie Anderson, the younger Tavener, folk singers plus pipes and hurdy-gurdies, Aboriginal musicians plus flutes and drums, Hawkwind.

All of them go into Hockley wood, near the shallow lake, and sometimes you can hear music. On their return they are debriefed at length before being bused to their hotel, exhausted and frightened, and sworn to secrecy.

April '94 (postcard)
Two of the writers have vanished: just their clothes found, oddly intertwined, plus a few frantically scribbled sentences from each, nothing coherent, although in the man's case, startlingly enigmatic. They'll be greatly missed by their fans.

Late April '94 (scrawled letter)
... A great deal of consternation. Rumor has it that something in the charisma of the wood is functioning in a way that was not expected. Each day, the stretch-limo brings the Charisma Source, the only man who can control his inadvertent creation. Master of the Id! In the Dancing Poachers, the talk is all of the stars "spinning and swirling above Hockley, like a heavenly whirlpool" a phenomenon witnessed by several local – and sober – people, although the effect lasted for just a few seconds.

A friend in the department of paleontology at Cambridge, someone who's always on the case in his quiet manner, has slipped me a note: new studies of bone fragments, collected in Victorian times from pits and excavations in the Hockley area that probably reached, during the digging, to levels representing fifty to one hundred thousand years Before Present, seem to be of *modern man*. Something about the teeth; lacunae in two molars show signs of having been produced by a metal drill! Sounds like one of those urban myths, doesn't it? But there's a real buzz of activity in the department. *Someone's taking it seriously.*

By the way, I see *you've* been invited to participate, along with others on the new list. Let me know when you're coming to Hockley.

May '94 (letter)
... It's Hawking's! The charisma DNA, I mean. The Cambridge mathematician who has visualized so much of the beginning of the universe. It's Hawking himself who arrives each day in the stretch-limo. He's trying to reverse the defensive field of the charisma trees at Hockley, to make them bring back the lives that have been set adrift in time!

It was so obvious, I suppose. Hawking's charisma is substantially related to his imagination, and his total engagement with Imaginative Time, an expression that turns out to be *his* coinage. The hazel wood has formed a tunnel from the beginning to the end of the universe as it exists for the *wood,* and they use it, as do all the *Corylus* woods, to protect themselves, not understanding – how can they? They are not sentient – that they are destroying life.

May '94 (postcard)
One of the writers who disappeared three weeks ago has returned, grotesquely naked and disheveled, aged by many

years, his flesh hanging from him in fatty rags. He stumbled from the wood clutching a strange flower, and was hastened away to the interview rooms to tell his story. I hear that he is insisting on "going back" — he's met someone — but he will not say to where. Something has happened to him and he no longer belongs in his own time. But he has been through the tunnel and survived! I hear talk that it is the trees *themselves* that have brought him back and sent him as an envoy, an emissary, to communicate with Hawking about what must be done to protect human life, while the imagination is allowed to access the views of past and future inside the hazel wood. Perhaps sentience exists after all!

June '94 (scrawled letter on back of manuscript sheet)
Rob — This may be my last letter — not sure — Phil has found a way through the military fence. We're going into Hockley wood tonight. It's an opportunity that we have to take — I can't explain it except to say it *feels* right. I'm drawn to Hockley. Charisma? Of course. But I don't want to think too rationally at the moment, I just need to hold Phil's hand and enter the flow of time. I know you're coming up soon, but I really can't wait for you. I have to go *now* into the flow.

By all the signs, that flow is *backwards,* and to that time of the intriguing forest fire, which I now think was probably started by the first unwilling travelers, the

Nighthawks. I want to come back, of course, but... well, there's no guaranteeing. How to communicate with you from so far in the past I haven't a clue, unless I scratch a letter on *ivory*. I'm prompted to suggest this by something Phil heard from the Nighthawks, way back, when they tried to kill him. They'd been over the Hockley area pretty thoroughly, but mostly Bad Finds; and the Bad Finds included a stack of bones with what looked like writing on them, which they assumed were some "freak show" and were disposed of.

If you ever locate Bad Find Pit, search among those bones for a letter from Rebecca.

I hope you don't get asked for postage!

∼

Rob Holdstock's penultimate words to me were: "I'll be in touch in July." I'm still waiting to hear from him.

Somehow or other.

David Garnett
Three Chimneys
Ferring
September 1994

THE AUTHORS

ROBERT HOLDSTOCK was born in Kent, where the marshes and woodlands were his childhood haunts. He had a Master's degree in Medical Zoology, and worked in medical research, before becoming a full-time writer in 1976. In 1984, he won the BSFA and World Fantasy Awards for Best Novel for *Mythago Wood*. It and the subsequent 'mythago' novels (including *Lavondyss*, which won the BSFA Award for Best Novel) cemented his reputation as the definitive portrayer of the wild wood. Celtic and Nordic mythology was also a consistent theme in his work including the 'Merlin Codex' trilogy (*Celtika*, *The Iron Grail* and *The Broken Kings*). Holdstock died in 2009, just four months after the publication of *Avilion*, the long-awaited and sadly final, return to Ryhope Wood (*Mythago Wood*).

> 'No other author has so successfully captured the magic of the wildwood.' – Michael Moorcock
>
> 'Sonorous, vivid and utterly enthralling' – *Times Literary Supplement*
>
> 'A writer of unusual delicacy and imagination' – *Observer*
>
> 'Beautifully paced ... a profoundly imaginative and remarkable book' – Alex de Jonge in the *Spectator*

www.robertholdstock.com
www.facebook.com/robertholdstockauthor

GARRY KILWORTH is still writing half a century from his first published piece of writing, a short poem on a Chinese warrior. He lives in East Anglia, but travels a great deal in the Far East. His latest publications are *The Iron Wire*, an historical novel set around the 1871 Adelaide to Darwin Telegraph Line, and *The Fabulous Beast*, a collection of horror, fantasy and science fiction tales, both published by Infinity Plus Books. In1992 he won the Children's Book Award with his fantasy novel *The Electric Kid* and in 2008 the Charles Whiting Award for Literature with his historical war novel *Rogue Officer*.

> 'The best short story I have read for many years' – JG Ballard on 'Sumi Dreams of a Paper Frog'

> 'A masterpiece of balanced and enigmatic storytelling … Kilworth has mastered the form.' – *Times Literary Supplement* on *In The Country Of Tattooed Men*

> 'Garry Kilworth is arguably the finest writer of short fiction today, in any genre.' – *New Scientist*

www.garry-kilworth.co.uk
www.facebook.com/GarryKilworth

ACKNOWLEDGEMENTS

'The Ragthorn' was first published in *A Whisper of Blood* edited by Ellen Datlow (Morrow Books) 1991.

'The Fabulous Beast' was first published in the short story collection of the same title published by Infinity Plus Books, 2013.

'The Charisma Trees' was first published in *New Worlds 4* edited by David Garnett (Gollancz) 1994.

MORE FROM INFINITY PLUS

On my way to Samarkand
memoirs of a travelling writer
by Garry Douglas Kilworth
http://www.infinityplus.co.uk/book.php?book=gkiomwts

Garry (Douglas) Kilworth is a varied and prolific writer who has travelled widely since childhood, living in a number of countries, especially in the Far East.

His books include science fiction and fantasy, historical novels, literary novels, short story collections, children's books and film novelisations.

This autobiography contains anecdotes about his farm worker antecedents and his rovings around the globe, as well as his experiences in the middle list of many publishing houses.

The style is chatty, the structure loose – pole vaulting time and space on occasion - and the whole saga is an entertaining ramble through a 1950s childhood, foreign climes and the genre corridors of the literary world.

> 'Kilworth is one of the most significant writers in the English language.' – *Fear*
>
> 'A convincing display of fine talent.' – *The Times* on *A Theatre Of Timesmiths*
>
> 'Kilworth is a master of his trade.' – *Punch*

For full details of infinity plus books
see www.infinityplus.co.uk

Made in the USA
Charleston, SC
27 September 2015